Acclaim
Wicked A

"Jourdan's *Wicked Angels* is a must-read for any serious student of queer studies. It is a fascinating representation of the early homoerotic novel. The controversy surrounding its censorship (a drama within itself) is also historically significant.

The fact that Armbrecht is himself a writer is an advantage and is clearly reflected in this engaging and unexpurgated translation. He injects a healthy dose of modernity and lucidity, yet allows the author's voice to remain audible. Translating Jourdan's highly visceral and descriptive prose was no easy task. If a good translation is an art, Armbrecht is a master. As important is Armbrecht's erudite and intriguing introduction, which so beautifully sets the psychosocial condition and describes the Zeitgeist during which the novel was created."

—Dr. Frederic B. Tate, PhD
Psychologist, Eastern State Hospital,
Williamsburg, VA

"First published in 1955 and promptly banned the following year, Eric Jourdan's book *Wicked Angels* is the story of adolescent love between two young men. Recounted in lyrical yet surprisingly explicit prose, the relationship is depicted at many levels, engaging sex, love, family dynamics, and social intercourse. Officially unavailable for almost thirty years, the novel was republished in 1985 and it has gotten well-deserved attention since then. With this excellent, faithful, and smooth translation, Thomas Armbrecht has brought this important book to English-speaking readers. His timely introduction places the book—tame by today's standards—in its social, historical, and cultural context. In providing this translation, Professor Armbrecht offers the public a romantic, yet frank, period piece that, in its directness, is a precursor to the culture of gay liberation that would become visible about fifteen years later."

—Lawrence R. Schehr, PhD
Professor of French,
University of Illinois

"This translation of Eric Jourdan's *Wicked Angels* by Thomas Armbrecht is preceded by an excellent introduction concerning French censorship in general and of this novel in particular.

Wicked Angels is a small jewel of a novel that needed a fresh translation. Contemporary readers will not feel the same sense of shock, scandal, and outrage that surrounded its first appearance on the French literary scene in 1955.

It is a classic love story of romance and tragedy. Pierre and Gerard can join Romeo and Juliet and Tristan and Isolde in the kingdom of absolute and deadly love. These young, beautiful, upper-class boys will know, dissect, and experience every aspect of love even and especially through blood and violence. The eternal and futile pursuit to become one can lead only to death and, in this case, as a rather lucid choice. The serene beauty of the Loire region contrasts with the violence of Pierre and Gerard's emotions and becomes an essential element in the story.

Neither homosexuality nor sadomasochism are new to literature, but what makes this book truly unique is the quality, the power, and the beauty of Eric Jourdan's prose. Mr. Armbrecht's excellent translation remains close to the original text, preserving the force, the strength, and richness of Jourdan's classical style.

It is for these reasons that this book will attract and captivate many readers."

—Professor Emerita María T. Robredo, AB, MA
French Section,
Department of Modern Languages & Literatures,
College of William & Mary

"*Wicked Angels* is a cannibalistic feast for the senses. The story of two adolescent cousins' passionate love for each other is told not through words, but through smells, tastes, and pulsating flesh. The cousins escape to a world of flowing water and body fluids, where the boundaries of pleasure and pain are blurred, where time is suspended and the present is all there is. The boys are two halves of a whole, whose desperate need to fuse can only be satisfied by turning their bodies inside out. They are trapped in a game of desire where there can be no winner, since the only path to freedom is through mutual self-destruction.

It is no surprise that this book was censored until 1985. Adult civility is exposed as pathetically impotent in the face of instinct, poetry, and youth. This is an obvious menace to the social order."

—Scott Gunther, PhD
Assistant Professor of French,
Wellesley College,
Department of French

NOTES FOR PROFESSIONAL LIBRARIANS AND LIBRARY USERS

This is an original book title published by Southern Tier Editions™, Harrington Park Press®, an imprint of The Haworth Press, Inc. Unless otherwise noted in specific chapters with attribution, materials in this book have not been previously published elsewhere in any format or language.

CONSERVATION AND PRESERVATION NOTES

All books published by The Haworth Press, Inc. and its imprints are printed on certified pH neutral, acid-free book grade paper. This paper meets the minimum requirements of American National Standard for Information Sciences-Permanence of Paper for Printed Material, ANSI Z39.48-1984.

DIGITAL OBJECT IDENTIFIER (DOI) LINKING

The Haworth Press is participating in reference linking for elements of our original books. (For more information on reference linking initiatives, please consult the CrossRef Web site at www.crossref.org.) When citing an element of this book such as a chapter, include the element's Digital Object Identifier (DOI) as the last item of the reference. A Digital Object Identifier is a persistent, authoritative, and unique identifier that a publisher assigns to each element of a book. Because of its persistence, DOIs will enable The Haworth Press and other publishers to link to the element referenced, and the link will not break over time. This will be a great resource in scholarly research.

Wicked Angels

HARRINGTON PARK PRESS®
Southern Tier Editions™

Titles of Related Interest

Lost Gay Novels: A Reference Guide to Fifty Works from the First Half of the Twentieth Century by Anthony Slide

Ambidextrous: The Secret Lives of Children by Felice Picano

Men Who Loved Me by Felice Picano

A House on the Ocean, a House on the Bay by Felice Picano

Aura by Gary Glickman

The Handsomest Man in the World by David Leddick

That Man from C.A.M.P. by Victor J. Banis

The Tomcat Chronicles: Erotic Adventures of a Gay Liberation Pioneer by Jack Nichols

Whose Eye Is on Which Sparrow? by Robert Taylor

Life, Sex, and the Pursuit of Happiness: A Novel by Fritz Klein

Some Dance to Remember: A Memoir-Novel of San Francisco 1970-1982 by Jack Fritscher

The Millionaire of Love by David Leddick

Wicked Angels

Eric Jourdan

Thomas J. D. Armbrecht
Translator

Southern Tier Editions™
Harrington Park Press®
An Imprint of The Haworth Press, Inc.
New York • London • Oxford

For more information on this book or to order, visit
http://www.haworthpress.com/store/product.asp?sku=5402

or call 1-800-HAWORTH (800-429-6784) in the United States and Canada
or (607) 722-5857 outside the United States and Canada

or contact orders@HaworthPress.com

Published by

Southern Tier Editions™, Harrington Park Press®, an imprint of The Haworth Press, Inc., 10 Alice Street, Binghamton, NY 13904-1580.

© 2006 by Thomas J. D. Armbrecht. All rights reserved. No part of this work may be reproduced or utilized in any form or by any means, electronic or mechanical, including photocopying, microfilm, and recording, or by any information storage and retrieval system, without permission in writing from the publisher. Printed in the United States of America.

PUBLISHER'S NOTES
The development, preparation, and publication of this work has been undertaken with great care. However, the Publisher, employees, editors, and agents of The Haworth Press are not responsible for any errors contained herein or for consequences that may ensue from use of materials or information contained in this work. The Haworth Press is committed to the dissemination of ideas and information according to the highest standards of intellectual freedom and the free exchange of ideas. Statements made and opinions expressed in this publication do not necessarily reflect the views of the Publisher, Directors, management, or staff of The Haworth Press, Inc., or an endorsement by them.

This is a work of fiction. Names, characters, places, and incidents either are the products of the author's imagination or are used fictitiously, and any resemblance to actual persons, living or dead, business establishments, events, or locales is entirely coincidental.

Cover credit: "Noonday Heat" by Henry Scott Tuke, RA, RWS, 1858-1929, reproduced by permission of The Royal Cornwall Polytechnic Society. Prints are available from the Society at 24 Church Street, Falmouth, Cornwall TR11 3EG, UK.

Cover design by Marylouise E. Doyle.

Library of Congress Cataloging-in-Publication Data

Jourdan, Eric.
   [Mauvais anges. English]
   Wicked angels / Eric Jourdan; Thomas J. D. Armbrecht, translator.
     p. cm.
   Includes bibliographical references.
   ISBN-13: 978-1-56023-548-4 (pbk. : alk. paper)
   ISBN-10: 1-56023-548-9 (pbk. : alk. paper)
   I. Armbrecht, Thomas J. D. II. Title.

PQ2670.09757M3813 2006
843'.914—dc22

2005023278

Introduction . . . vii
Thomas J. D. Armbrecht

Part One: Pierre's Story

    I . . . 1

    II . . . 11

    III . . . 23

    IV . . . 38

    V . . . 47

    VI . . . 56

Part Two: Gerard's Story

    I . . . 63

    II . . . 78

    III . . . 87

    IV . . . 97

    V . . . 111

Introduction

Wicked Angels and Censorship

> Transgression is not the negation of the taboo; it goes beyond it and completes it.
>
> Georges Bataille, *L'Erotisme* (1957)

In the minds of most people, France is a country synonymous with freedom, particularly sexual and literary freedom. Although this is not exactly a misconception, like most countries, France has known periods of conservatism, during which certain forms of self-expression were controlled and even punished. Originally published in 1955, but censored until 1985, Eric Jourdan's novel *Wicked Angels (Les mauvais anges)* was a victim of such repression.[1] The book's prohibition, coupled with the homosexual themes that earned it such a distinction, makes *Wicked Angels* an important part of the history of French literature and publishing. A product of its time and circumstance, readers must understand not only why the novel was censored but also why it was written in order to appreciate it as more than just a titillating or shocking tale.

France had known periods of extreme censorship prior to the twentieth century. Before the French Revolution, some 40 percent of all prisoners incarcerated in the Bastille were there because of book-related crimes (Netz, 1997, p. 45). In the mid-eighteenth century, both Flaubert and Baudelaire underwent famous trials for *Madame Bovary* and *Les Fleurs du mal* (respectively), the latter of which was condemned because its "crude realism was an offense to decency" (cited in Ono-dit-Biot, 2002, p. 88).[2] After obscenity laws were revised in 1881, however, France had such liberal policies that it was thought to be "unique in the world" in its attitudes toward freedom of expression (Joubert, 2001, p. 7). The original and daring books published between World War I and World War II by authors such as Henry Miller, Jean Cocteau, and André Gide (to name but a few) attest to the lack of restrictions of that period.

Antebellum liberty was followed by what has been called a period of "extreme censorship" that lasted until the end of the 1960s (Phillips, 1999, p. 16). Ironically, it was brought about by the supposedly liberal, leftist government that enacted "Law number 49-956, Regarding Publications Destined for Youth" on July 16, 1949. Although it followed a long tradition of legislation designed to protect the general public from licentious materials, the law of 1949 was remarkable because, unlike its predecessors and contrary to what its name implied, it covered not only materials published particularly for young people, but also, as specified in article 14, included "publications of all sorts that [were] dangerous to youth because of their licentious or pornographic character, because they depict[ed] crime, violence or racial hatred, or because they encourage[d] the use, possession or traffic of drugs" (cited in Crepin and Groensteen, 1999, p. 12). This meant that almost any document, whether printed or filmed, could be censored, regardless of its intended audience.

The censorship law of 1949 was meant in part as a response to the effects of Nazi propaganda (hence its prohibition against inciting racial hatred), and to a lesser extent, as a way of controlling the influx of American popular media (especially comic books, which regularly depicted gangsters and "bestial men" like Tarzan). Considered as a reaction to these common enemies, it is understandable that the law attracted widespread support that transcended traditional political and ideological lines. As a result, "The Committee to Survey and Control Published Works Destined for Children and Adolescents" (informally known as "La Commission du Livre," or "The Book Board") was formed with a heterogeneous mix of government officials, Communists, and even Catholic clergy. The binding force among such a diverse and potentially self-antagonizing group was undoubtedly a common agreement on the vulnerability of children. It is hardly surprising, therefore, that the Book Board also targeted texts dealing with homosexual pedophilia, the bête noire of parents and menace of children, par excellence.

In a far-reaching move similar to their decision to censor not only books written for children, but any document that might negatively affect a child, the committee decided to ban books not only about homosexuality, but also those that depicted homosexuals in even a mildly favorable light. This sentiment was made official in a decision from the "Thibault" case of 1956, which declared that the term *licentious* covered "not only that which is indecent, but also that which is against the established order *(déréglé)*. Homosexuality is licentious. To make apologies for this vice is, therefore, to act licentiously" (Crepin and Groensteen, 1999, p. 13). The use of the adjective *déréglé* (literally, "unruly" or "out of order") reveals the true nature of government officials' fear of homosexuality: they viewed it as a destabilizing force that threatened the very *bonnes moeurs* ("good morals" or standards of decency) that held society together, the concept of which formed the "basis of all censorship laws in France" throughout the twentieth century (Phillips, 1999, p. 15). As Senator Joseph Sigrist stated in defense of the policy: "If youth is perverted, it will lose all taste for marriage. Even if it still maintains an interest, it will no longer understand the sacred duties of marriage that demand that one bear children for the nation and the homeland" (Poulain, 1998, p. 559). As literary historian Bernard Joubert (2001) has pointed out in his *Erotic Anthology of Censorship (Anthologie érotique de la censure)*, "it doesn't come as any surprise that The Book Board was profoundly homophobic during its first two decades of operation" (p. 179); in their minds, they were protecting not only the children, but the very existence of French civilization.

In point of fact, it would perhaps be more accurate to write that the Book Board was protecting *"middle*-class civilization," because it wasn't uniformly concerned with all French citizens. The committee was careful to distinguish between books that would be available only to a particular audience of intellectuals (who were apparently immune to their nefarious effects) and books intended for the general public. In a very famous case involving the publication of the works of the Marquis de Sade, the editor Jean-Jacques Pauvert (1957) argued that the books were intended for a particular audience of "doctors, philosophers and scholars of literature, who would use them to learn about psychological problems necessary to their work. [. . . The publication would be] restricted, scientific, expensive and intended only for selected readers" (p. 114). The court apparently accepted this argument because, although the books were banned for the general public, they were also found to have sufficient artistic value to justify their conservation and therefore "ordered by the Court to be deposited at the National Library" (Poulain, 1998, p. 569).

A similar dichotomy occurred in 1950 with Jean Genet's novel and poem, *Querelle de Brest* and *La Galère*, respectively. Pierre Descaves, speaking as a representative of The Society of Men of Letters stated, "The fact that this is a deluxe edition published in very limited number along with the hermetism that characterizes Jean Genet's poem could, if necessary, make it appear devoid of all danger to *bonnes moeurs*" (cited in Poulain, 1998, p. 567). In this particular case, this line of argumentation did not work, and Genet was condemned to prison for eight months. As soon as the following year (1953), however, Gallimard, one of the most intellectual and prestigious publishers of the day, published an edition of his complete works. Even more ironically, the decision regarding the aforementioned works was overturned in 1956, the same year Jourdan's *Wicked Angels* was banned. Seemingly, if one's work was classified as intellectual or esteemed by the elite, then the concept of *bonnes moeurs* did not apply.

As he himself has stated, Jourdan is convinced that the principal reason his book was censored was because it is the story of two upper-middle class adolescents, and was therefore perceived to be particularly subversive (personal interview, June 9, 2004). Indeed, there are several passages in *Wicked Angels* in which the protagonists express disgust with the repressive society around them and act out against it. Pierre frequently questions the importance of education, and refuses to study: "Screw homework. I'm against what they're trying to make me learn, anyway. Youth should mean freedom. They're trying to get us to live our whole lives in captivity, until our skin becomes the color of the paper of our books. I won't do it! I won't!" (p. 55). He has failed the French *baccalauréate* exam, the sine qua non of bourgeois respectability, but is completely unrepentant. Gerard, too, is clear about his opinion of society's values: "Society made me sick with its stupid prejudices, its respectability. I resented people trying to assert the principles that they had constructed on life's emptiness" (p. 156). It is as if the two boys personify the Book Board's worst nightmare, and they haven't even made reference to their sexuality!

As these passages suggest, it is plausible that *Wicked Angels* was censored as much for flying in the face of *bonnes moeurs* as for being obscene or licentious. As the rest of this analysis shows, however, the characters and subject matter of the novel are not the only subversive element of the novel; its narrative style and structure are, as well. This idea is supported by two documents included with the text when it was originally published that seem to anticipate several possible objections. Before turning to the text itself to see which, if any, of the Book Board's crimes it was guilty of, an analysis of the book's presentation reveals as much about its form and content as do the Book Board's actions. By analyzing the preemptive defense of the novel, in the form of these two appendixes, we can better understand not only interpretations of the text in its historical context, but also mid-century strategies for countering censorship.

In defense of his work *The New Justine,* the Marquis de Sade included the following quote on the frontispiece: "One is hardly criminal for depicting the bizarre penchants that nature inspires" *("On n'est point criminel pour faire la peinture/des bizarres penchants qu'inspire la nature").* This verse wittily argues that artistic realism is self-justifying. It also implies that the artist's primary responsibility is "to paint" *("faire la peinture"),* and that it is therefore for his artistic abilities—not the work's "realistic" content—that he should be judged. As Phillips (1999) points out in his book on censorship, *Forbidden Fictions,* the notions of realism and "artistic value" were often used to defend works of art in the 1950s and 1960s (p. 2). This seemingly explains why the original publication of *Wicked Angels* included two appendixes from well-known authors defending the work on just these grounds, undoubtedly in anticipation of negative reactions to its subject matter. The first, a letter to the editor from prolific writer and cultural critic Max-Pol Fouchet, insists on the work's truthful representation of love. He claims that Pierre and Gerard's passion is archetypically adolescent, remarking that, "The world of 'grown-ups' is as far from them as Betelgeuse is from a sea-cucumber" (Jourdan, [1955] 2001, p. 187). By differentiating their love in this way, Fouchet makes a claim for its veracity; if it seems unorthodox or incredible, that's because it is outside the realm of adult relationships. He is careful, however, not to denigrate their ardor just because the lovers are both male. In fact, he situates it in a long line of violent love stories when he writes, "The two boys . . . belong to the race of Tristan and Isolde, of Romeo and Juliet" (p. 188), an idea also voiced by Pierre in the first chapter of part two of the novel. In this way, Fouchet retraces the argument used by Sade, showing that the boys' sadistic love is not only plausible but part of a tradition familiar to (and admired by) the bourgeois audience it is likely to offend. He concludes by arguing that *Wicked Angels* ultimately "transcends uranism [homosexuality]," and declares flatly that "no book is further from 'vice'" (p. 189), thereby attempting to secure its status as art-inspired-by-nature.

Novelist Robert Margerit wrote the text found in the second appendix included with the original version of *Wicked Angels*. He takes a similar tactic, even going so far as to claim that Jourdan's description of homosexual love will teach the heterosexual reader something: "Isn't it, in effect, thanks to the abnormal that morality is explained? The exception makes the plain the rule" (Jourdan, [1955] 2001, p. 191). Yourcenar ([1939] 1982) supports this by insisting on the book's artistic merit, thereby taking up Sade's second line of defense: "The gifts of the writer, his astonishing ability to restore brilliant originality and novelty to everything that his pen touches (particularly to something as hackneyed as love), will amaze the reader" (p. 190). In other words, it is Jourdan's remarkable writing, as much as it is the book's unusual subject matter, that allows him to say something new about love, a subject of interest to almost all readers. Margerit stresses the author's "exceptional poetic gift" (p. 191) as he describes the book's worth, seemingly in direct anticipation of the types of criticism it was likely to encounter.

These same arguments against censorship were further developed by *Tel Quel*, a group of literary and cultural critics that was interested in what scholar Nicholas Harrison (1995) has called "the subversive potential of creative writing" (p. 122). In an essay on Sade called "Sade, Fourier, Loyola" published in 1971, *Tel Quel* member Roland Barthes claimed that most books that were subject to censorship were subversive in artistic, rather than moral, ways:

> The most profound subversion (counter censorship) doesn't necessarily consist in saying something that will shock public opinion and morals, the law, or the police, but rather in inventing a paradoxical discourse (free from all *doxa* [from Gr. Δοζα: opinion]): invention (and not provocation) is a revolutionary act that can only be accomplished in the founding of a new language. Sade's grandeur didn't come from celebrating crime and perversion, or from having used radical language for this celebration. It came instead from inventing a vast discourse. (p. 812)

Although Barthes never wrote about Jourdan's *Wicked Angels,* one can conclude that he would have agreed with Margerit's opinion that much of the book's value came from the originality of its expression. He might have gone even further, however, and said that it was this very originality that made it seem so subversive to its critics. In his foreword to a recent edition of *Les mauvais anges* published by Editions La Musardine in 2001, Pauvert echoes this idea by claiming that Jean Pihan, an abbot in the Catholic Church and the head of the Book Board, was particularly concerned by "the danger that the ambiguity that these 'special friendships' *("amitiés particulières")* represented when presented by such a skilled dissimulator. An ambiguity that was in his eyes one hundred times worse than the most explicit obscenity" (2001, p. 9). The ambiguity and dissimulation that the priest fears is essentially a result of Jourdan's lyricism. Its beauty and originality attracts (or in Father Pihan's mind, distracts) the reader from the nefarious subject matter. Thus, following Barthes's line of thought, Jourdan's work is subversive since, like Sade's, it privileges the signifier (poetic language) over the signified (Pierre and Gerard's violent homosexual relationship).[3]

Now that the historical and social contexts in which *Wicked Angels* was written are clearer, it is time to turn to the text itself to see how Eric Jourdan created a book so "dangerous" that it was banned for almost thirty years. What follows is an analysis of various narrative tropes used in the book to demonstrate that the author was as interested in challenging ideas of normality as he was in writing about homosexuality, and that he did so as much through the language that he used as through the subject that he chose. Considered in this light, contemporary readers can appreciate a work that might otherwise appear grandiloquent and possibly even homophobic, given the violent deaths of the two main characters at the end.

For a story about two adolescents in love, a fair number of sexual acts are described.[4] More surprising, perhaps, is the remarkable amount of sensuality in the text; everything is erotically charged—the trees, the air, the smallest touch, or even a glance between the boys—because of the level of detail with which it is described. Even the opening scene of the text, in which Pierre watches Gerard nap, turns the boy's slumber into an erotic experience for the viewer:

> Legs spread, a tuft of pale yellow soapwort against his knees, Gerard slept. His half-opened shirt seemed to be a white wave breaking on the honey-colored dome of his chest. My eyes followed the muscles of his throat toward the neckline of his collar. Their force seemed to emphasize the contrasting softness of the shadows near his shoulder. (p. 15)

This is typical of Jourdan's writing in that it describes an unexceptional action with an attention to detail that elevates to the level of the poetic, while avoiding facile vulgarity. Although none of the words in Jourdan's lexicon could be considered euphemistic or even allusive, they communicate the narrator's desire clearly.

Jourdan's ability to eroticize without being crude is remarkable because it successfully tackles one of the principal challenges faced by anyone who wrote about homosexuality before there was a real precedent for doing so. As Yourcenar ([1939] 1982), a French writer celebrated for her elegance and erudition, wrote in the introduction to her novel *Alexis,* authors dealing with same-sex love face particular linguistic difficulties:

> The writer who wants to [write of a character's homosexuality] honestly, eliminating from his language the supposedly "decent" formulas of facile literature that are in reality half-timid and half-licentious, has a choice of only two or three means of expression that are all more or less defective and unacceptable. The terms from scientific vocabulary . . . are only of value for specialized works, for which they were coined: these word-labels go against literature, which is individuality in expression. Obscenity . . . remains an exterior solution: the hypocritical reader tends to accept the incongruous word like a Pittoresque form, or almost like exoticism. . . . Obscenity gets old very quickly. (p. 4)

Even when recounting actions that are overtly sexual, Jourdan still avoids the obscene by maintaining a level of formality in his tone that stands in contrast with the rawness of what he is describing. He frequently relies on textual devices common to poetry, such as metaphor, unusual syntax, and a close attention to the sound of words. In the following passage, in which Pierre beats Gerard during what starts as a game and then progresses to something more serious, the author subtly employs unorthodox sentence structure and personification, and pays close attention to the sound of the words he chooses. The text is also noteworthy because of the exacting observations of the narrator, who cerebrally analyzes his behavior even as he executes it:

> What troubled jealousy I displayed in this taste for hurting him exactly where I admired him the most! I didn't undress him, because my blows hurt all the more through his clothes. I would have been afraid that I might give in to my basest hungers too quickly, had he been naked. . . .
>
> I hit him again and again. First came the long whistle of admiration from the belt, then the flat sound of the blow with which the sound of my erratic breathing mixed. Gerard stopped breathing, groaning in pain even before contact with the belt. He only

> gasped afterward, if the poorly aimed blow had hit bare skin. . . . A vein swelled on the back of his knee, but disappeared each time he gave into this painful pleasure. I found nothing sweeter than caressing him there, putting my lips on the spot for the briefest moment. (p. 94)

Jourdan's description does not include any mention of traditionally sexual activities or organs, nor does it employ any vocabulary that could be considered licentious. The author's inventiveness and, in the minds of the Book Board at least, his wickedness, come from his ability to eroticize body parts that are not usually associated with sex through descriptions that are as frank as they are titillating.

Wicked Angels' lyricism is complemented by the use of many allusions to classical literature. Although these references occupy a justifiable place in the text, since both boys are studying Latin at school, they nevertheless lend a learned air to the work (and consequently to the author, as well). Figures from history are often used as a kind of shorthand. For example, Gerard describes a disagreement with his father about an upcoming vacation as a classical tragedy in which he assigns each of his family members a role:

> I would remain in Paris with them, while my cousin would take Pierre to Italy. . . . My father would play Burrhus to Pierre's father's Seneca, and they would take turns looking after me, the young Nero. Pierre, on the other hand, would retire to the home of some vestal virgin or other. (p. 111)

The uncommented mention of these historical personages implies that the reader knows that Burrhus and Seneca were Nero's educators and protectors when he was young, but were ultimately unable to control him as an adult. The allusion functions as a sort of half-joke, hyperbolically elevating Pierre and Gerard's conflict with their fathers to the level of tragedy, while at the same time linking their trials to a literary tradition.

Toward the end of the story, Jourdan uses actual passages from famous books in order to underscore the intractable nature of the boys' fate. After a series of ominous presentiments, Gerard decides to open books at random in order to find out what will happen to him and Pierre. First he grabs Shakespeare's *Romeo and Juliet,* presumably a schoolbook, and, closing his eyes, opens the book and points his finger at the text. Not liking the passage he finds, he turns next to Dante's *Inferno* and finally to the Bible, which frighten and confuse him in turn. The primary function of the quotes from all three texts is to foreshadow what happens at the end of the book. A secondary but equally important purpose is, however, to reinforce the significance of what happens to the boys; like Romeo and Juliet, Pierre and Gerard's love is preordained, if star-crossed. In fact, the disastrous end foretold by each of the books ennobles their fate by firmly inscribing it in the genre of tragedy, whose function according to Aristotle's *Poetics* is, it will be remembered, to instruct by demonstrating the noble behavior of heroic characters. Jourdan's use of these classic texts makes it clear that he is inviting the reader to view the boys' downfall as the result of their hubris, and not as the outcome of their "vice."

This pedagogical aspect of *Wicked Angels* is reinforced by the abundance of aphorisms within it. Even though the protagonists are both teenagers, they often make pronouncements containing some general truth that is potentially relevant outside its immediate context. These are readily identifiable because they usually concern universal concepts such as beauty, destiny, or love, and do not make specific reference to any of the characters in the text, as in the following examples proclaimed by both Pierre and Gerard:

- Destiny needs time to play itself out! (p. 47)
- A lover hates time, since it is always stealing the one he loves from him. (p. 74)
- At seventeen you have the force, but not the means to fight. (p. 112)
- Beauty is always important, even in cases of desperation. (p. 116)

A work filled with maxims automatically seems more important, since it subscribes to the *quod semper, quod ubique, quod ab omnibus* notion, often associated with "great" literature, that it contains ideas that will always be pertinent to everyone everywhere. Without presuming that Jourdan intended his novel to have a wide-ranging philosophical relevance, his use of aphorisms makes the book potentially relevant not just to homosexuals, but to anyone interested in love, since he writes of it in a universal sense for which the boys' experiences are just possible examples. Jourdan is not the only author writing of homosexuality to use this literary device; writers such as the aforementioned Yourcenar have used maxims to similar effect in works about the subject (see, for example, her novels *Alexis* or *Memoires of Hadrien*). It is also interesting to note that although he does not mention this trope specifically, Margerit does bring up *Wicked Angels'* innovative treatment of love when defending Jourdan's subject matter, and claims that it was only through this risky choice that he could say anything new:

> Thanks to his exceptional subject, Eric Jourdan has dazzled us by finding a way to give new meaning to certain sentiments, desires, and acts whose marvelous nature hasn't been evident for quite some time. Everything wears out, love included. In order to restore brilliance to its storms, its caresses, the writer must look towards an exceptional passion in order to give love back its primitive virtues. (p. 191)

The frequent use of maxims in *Wicked Angels* could be viewed, therefore, as one of Jourdan's strategies for making the boys' love seem more like an illustration of all types of passionate love, independent of gender, and therefore more familiar (and acceptable) to all sorts of readers. To Father Pihan and the rest of the Book Board, Jourdan's universal message, communicated in such a lyrical way and aligned with so many canonical texts, would have seemed more seductive and more threatening to youths than the sex actually described in the book. One can therefore assume that the book was banned not because it was terribly licentious (particularly compared to authors such as Genet or Leduc), but because it *wasn't* so: the only thing that could be more dangerous than describing or apologizing for homosexuality would be normalizing it.

The novel's violence and symmetrical structure are two other, related aspects of *Wicked Angels* that destabilize the bourgeois milieu described in the book in a way that the Book Board must have found threatening. In "Masochism, Sadism and Homotextuality," one of the few critical articles dealing with any text by Jourdan,[5] Owen Heathcote suggests that the book's two-part structure and prevalent violence work together to throw into question some of the various binaries around which society organizes itself. He notes that, "[Pierre and Gerard's] exultantly male-to-male passion both intensifies and overturns their sense of sexuality, gender and identity, thereby creating irresolvable conflicts expressed in an appropriately two-voiced homotextual narrative" (1994, p. 181). In other words, the young men become increasingly violent as they struggle to maintain a sense of identity in the face of their increasing passion, which threatens them while bringing them closer together at the same time. It is true that as the violence in the book escalates, each boy voices with increasing frequency his desire not just to be with the other, but to *become* the other. As Gerard observes in the middle of a ritual in which the boys take turns cutting each other and drinking the blood in an attempt to mutually incorporate their essences,

> Pierre was more than just one person: we didn't know anymore where exactly my soul stopped and his began. Each day, I learned to live as him. We became so similar that, even though we didn't really look anything alike, people mistook us for each other because love had given us the same face. (p. 127)

As Heathcote (1994) points out, this urge to resemble each other is ultimately self-destructive, "firstly because merging with the other destroys the self, and secondly, because the urge to assimilate and possess the other also destroys the other" (p. 184). It is probable that Pierre and Gerard's suffocating rather was precisely the kind of "amitié particulière" that Father Pihan considered an unhealthy example when deciding to ban *Wicked Angels*.

Even the overall structure of the novel reflects Pierre and Gerard's simultaneous convergence and separation as manifested through their concurrently increasing affection and violence. Parts one and two recount essentially the same series of events, accentuating each boy's slightly different perspective in order to give a more complete picture. Despite this double narration, however, there is still an untethered quality to the text: flashbacks intermingle with real-time events; actual occurrences give way to fantasies almost seamlessly. Although this chronological and existential haziness doesn't quite equal the "temporal, spatial and narrative loopings and layerings" that Heathcote identifies as a form of *mise en abîme* in Jourdan's trilogy, *Charité, Révolte,* and *Sang,* its net effect of "showing the imbrication of masculinity and violence" is the same (p. 184). Jourdan communicates the desperate nature of the boys' desire for each other by showing both sides of the story. In this way, he anticipates the only possible resolution to the boys' situation, which is indeed how the book ends: "If death was the only force powerful enough to separate those whom destiny had united in an embrace, like two sides of the same coin or the two faces of Janus depicted on the gates of war, then death was the only way that either of us would ever liberate our souls" (p. 122). Pierre and Gerard are essentially two sides of the same coin that no mere mortal (including members of the Book Board) can separate. The symmetrical form of Jourdan's novel is a narrative reflection of the boys' relationship, and mirrors their physical and mental proximities in a tacitly subversive way.

Although it is unlikely that the Book Board was fully appreciative of Jourdan's efforts to get his message and his means to work in such harmony, *Wicked Angels* was evidently disturbing on enough levels that Father Pihan "knew pornography when he saw it," to paraphrase U.S. Justice Potter Stewart's infamous words about pornography from 1964. It is, however, a disservice to the work not to consider the textual strategies Jourdan uses to explore the doubly taboo subject of adolescent homosexuality and sadomasochism. Moreover, it is only by being cognizant of the historical context in which the novel was born that a contemporary reader can understand the author's stylistic choices and can appreciate the novel's subject matter in all its sensational glory. Even when the book first appeared in 1955, its tone may have been foreign to sympathetic readers, because, as Pierre remarks:

I was well aware that romantic sentiments were out of fashion. Heartfelt emotion was naive kitsch. I suppose that if I could have been more blasé about the whole thing, it would have seemed more natural and would have hidden our happiness. Loving another boy would have almost looked normal; we would have seemed like everybody else. In their eyes, however, any love that refuses to inhabit their world is not normal. (p. 136)

In other words, Jourdan's very project necessitated extreme means of expression because it was expressing the extreme. If the love it describes is "not normal," that is because it transcends more than just conceptions of gender; it subverts ideas about youth and class, as well. The novel is, however, as passionate—and as passionately recounted—as is any tale of ill-fated lovers. This lends it an emotional legitimacy that the Book Board must have found as true as it was terrifying.

NOTES

1. In addition to forbidding the publication of the book in 1956, Father Pihan, the head of the Book Board that censored the work, wanted to take Jourdan to court for "offending public decency." Jourdan was spared a trial thanks to the efforts of Paul Boncour (of the Société des Nations [the United Nations]) and Pierre Descaves (who was Jean Genet's lawyer). Jourdan's book was censored for a second time in 1974, after homosexuality had more or less ceased to be a reason for banning a text. Editor Jean-Jacques Pauvert has stated that the reason the book's interdiction was renewed was because no published edition of the text could be found (cited in Jourdan, 2001, p. 8). The committee making the decision decided that it would be a dangerous precedent to lift the sanction based solely on the manuscript because manuscripts can differ significantly from final versions. This argument seems rather specious and a possible cover for homophobia, however, since the publisher wanted simply to republish the work, and since the lack of any published edition was due to the work being censored by the committee in the first place!

2. All translations in text are mine unless otherwise stated. Page numbers are given for the work in the original language.

3. Many of the other writers who treated homosexuality in their works from this period are also well-known for their inventive lyrical style. Both Jean Genet and Violette Leduc's prose often borders on poetry, particularly when they are describing amorous and sexual acts.

4. One of the sexual episodes described in the first edition of *Wicked Angels* was considered by the publisher to be too daring. They cut some of the scene during which Gerard has sex with another boy in his car (Part 2, Chapter 3). The editor indicated the omission with twenty-five lines of white space (Eric Jourdan, personal interview, June 9, 2004).

5. Jourdan has published nine novels in France, none of which has been translated into English except *Les mauvais anges*. He is also a playwright and the author of prefaces to several volumes of the *Complete Works* of Académie Française member Julien Green. Green, who was one of twentieth-century France's most important and renowned writers, was Jourdan's father by adoption; the two collaborated on several projects early in Jourdan's career.

BIBLIOGRAPHY

Aristotle (350 BCE). Poetics. S. H. Butcher (trans.). Available online at http://classics.mit.edu/Aristotle/poetics.1.1.html.

Barthes, Roland. *Sade, Fourier, Loyola* (1971). *Oeuvres completes III: Livres, textes, entretiens 1968-1971*. (2002). In Eric Marty, ed. Paris: Seuil, 699-870.

Bataille, Georges ([1957] 1987). *L'Erotisme. Oeuvres Complètes X*. Paris: Gallimard. Introduction by Michel Foucault.

Crepin, Thierry and Thierry Groensteen (eds.) (1999). *"On tue à chaque page": La loi de 1949 sur les publications destinées à la jeunesse*. Paris: Editions du Temps/Musée de la Bande Dessinée.

de Sade, Marquis ([1799] 1958). *La Nouvelle Justine ou les malheurs de la vertu*. Jean Jacques Pauvert, ed. Paris: J. J. Pauvert. Available online, including frontispiece and illustrations, at http://www.univ-montp3.fr/~pictura/Serie.php ?notice=A0940.

Genet, Jean (1947). *La galère* . . . Paris: Jacques Loyau.

Genet, Jean (1953). *Querelle de Brest*. Paris: Gallimard.

Harrison, Nicholas (1995). *Circles of Censorship: Censorship and Its Metaphors in French History, Literature and Theory*. Oxford, England: Clarendon Press.

Heathcote, Owen (1994). Masochism, sadism and homotextuality. *Paragraph: A Journal of Modern Critical Theory* 17(4): 174-189.

Heathcote, Owen (1998). Jobs for the boys? Or: What's new about the male hunter in Duvert, Guibert and Jourdan. In Owen Heathcote, Alex Hughes, and James S. Williams, eds., *Gay Signatures: Gay and Lesbian Theory, Fiction and Film in France, 1945-1995* (pp. 173-192). Oxford and New York: Berg Publishing.

Joubert, Bernard (2001). *Anthologie érotique de la censure.* Paris: Editions de La Musardine.

Jourdan, Eric ([1955] 2001). *Les mauvais anges.* Paris: Editions de la Pensée Moderne. Paris: Editions de la Musardine. Appendixes by Max-Pol Fouchet and Robert Margerit, Introduction by Jean-Jacques Pauvert.

Netz, Robert (1997). *Histoire de la censure dans l'édition.* Paris: Presse Universitaires de France.

Ono-dit-Biot, Christophe (2002). Seche tes larmes, Eros. *Le Point* 1529 (January 4): 88.

Pauvert, Jean-Jacques (1957). Defendant. *L'affaire Sade compte-rendu exact de procès intenté par le Ministère public aux Éditions Jean-Jacques Pauvert contient notamment les temoignages de Georges Bataille, André Breton, Jean Cocteau, Jean Paulhan et le teste intégral de la plaidoire prononcée par Maurice Garcon.* Paris: J. J. Pauvert.

Phillips, John (1999). *Forbidden Fictions: Pornography and Censorship in Twentieth-Century French Literature.* Sterling, VA: Pluto Press.

Poulain, Martine (1998). La Censure. In Pascal Fouché, ed., *L'Edition française depuis 1945.* Paris: Editions du Cercle.

Yourcenar, Marguerite ([1939] 1982). *Alexis, ou le Traité du vain combat. Œuvres romanesques.* Paris: Gallimard.

Part One:
Pierre's Story

. . . Twist on their pillows the brown adolescents.

Baudelaire, "Morning Twilight," *The Flowers of Evil*

Pass us by and forgive us our happiness.

Dostoyevsky, *The Idiot*

I

The sky was a deep royal blue with a calm grandeur. You couldn't tell whether or not the sun was out. The water flowed under the plane trees and the silver birches without mirroring anything, reflecting only when a ray of sunlight traversed its shadowy green depths that in places darkened to black. Between the trees, the summer had scorched the tall grasses that fell all over the place like crazy golden hair. Through half-closed eyes, the countryside became gigantic.

Legs spread, a tuft of pale yellow soapwort against his knees, Gerard slept. His half-opened shirt seemed to be a white wave breaking on the honey-colored dome of his chest. My eyes followed the muscles of his throat toward the neckline of his collar. Their force seemed to emphasize the contrasting softness of the shadows near his shoulder. Except for one cheek, his face was hidden from me. His hair seemed mixed with blades of dried grass. Curls rolled on his forehead. In the hollow of his temple a heavy vein, swollen with the heat, brought the confused glow of blood to his cheek and lent this sleeping boy a voluptuousness more violent than the arrogance of his features, so evident when he was awake.

I would have liked to stop the day, to enshrine forever the elusive instant in the face of Gerard who slept at my knees. Each second brought the cruel dementia of the past to my breath, in the greenest tone of the trees, in the most solemn silence of the water. Gerard had a mean beauty that could be sensed, even when he was napping, thanks to the sock rolled halfway down his ankle that revealed the sinewy leg of a tree climber.

I thought back over our whole life together to those times when we'd been free of parents and guardians. Although it wasn't easy, I decided to block everything from my mind except today and the first hours of our vacation together. The morning had passed in my room. We were supposed to be doing homework. We were playing dice instead. As usual, lunch was a silent affair between his father, my own, and a female cousin who had been taking care of us since we had both lost our mothers, who had been sisters. When I say that lunches were silent, that's because I see them from our perspective. We sat opposite the adults, not paying attention to a thing they said. Eating with them always felt like a waste of time.

As we finished our meals, Gerard looked at me in an underhanded manner that would have seemed suspicious had anyone been paying attention. Once outside, he explained what he'd had in mind: "Let's go near the river to sleep in the grass, okay?" The river was actually just a stream between two ponds on our property. We called it a river because of its proximity to the Loire, which was farther on and which attracted us less since it belonged to everyone. We took our time getting there in order to avoid running into some annoying adult who might force us to go home before we felt like it.

Gerard tanned less quickly than did I, but he had caught up with me in a week. We were both so golden brown that girls and boys alike watched us pass when we went through town. They too had that beauty with which the outdoors and a tranquil life had adorned them, making a rose bloom under their tanned cheeks and giving their bodies the tranquil magnificence of youth. I had learned to understand their looks. At first they were surprised; then they linked us together, Gerard and me, in silent admiration. From that instant, we lived in their dreams. Our faces no longer belonged to us.

Gerard loved to take me by the arm as we walked. We kept looking at each other, as if nothing else existed. As soon as we were alone in the countryside, however, we separated, although we were unable to leave each other completely. Gerard walked silently with his head down. After a few minutes, I grew bored and tried to amuse myself by kicking stones. It ended up being horrible. Gerard threw his head back and squared his shoulders. His defiant look made me decide to act as if I didn't care a bit. We already loved each other without knowing it.

Our mutual desire to be indispensable to the other made it seem almost as if we were rivals. Each of us dreamed more than once of running away without saying anything. As soon as one of us had decided to spend the day alone, it so happened that the other, compelled by a feeling that he couldn't control, made some captivating gesture, like saying some word that bordered on love. Once again, we would both throw ourselves heart and soul into the servitude of presence.

That afternoon, we loitered on the road more than usual. The heat was so intense that it seemed to turn the landscape gray when the sun was at its strongest. Everyone else was indoors, trying to stay cool, which allowed us to take a detour to one of the ponds without being seen. Suddenly the afternoon belonged to us alone. We walked without a word under the cover of the trees. Everything around us was quiet as we ambled next to the steamy water. In one place, where young oak saplings and brambles were particularly thick, you had to push the leaves out of the way to see the river. I heard Gerard, his voice firm but low, like that of a boy whose heart is beating too fast, say: "Here is good; the sun has burned the grass. It's softer to lie down on . . . and we'll be completely alone." We found ourselves in a small clearing.

Gerard opened his shirt and lay down. I was too excited to say anything. He took his T-shirt, which he had taken off and stuck provocatively into his belt upon leaving the house, and put it under his head. He closed his eyes, pretending to be asleep. I also opened my shirt, which was sticking to my skin, and then knelt to take it off completely. Turning toward him, I saw that Gerard was examining me between his half-closed eyes. His look was so strange that I felt as though I had never been so naked, even though he saw me so in the bathroom every day. While getting dressed in front of each other, I often hung around half-dressed, in my underwear or even without any clothes, while we washed ourselves. On the banks of this river, modesty directed our gazes as we dried ourselves and put our jeans back on, our legs still wet. Like me, Gerard wasn't exactly unaware of the private parts of my body. He respected our discomfort, however, and didn't seek to see beyond those physical positions that the eye finds unsatisfying. With similar prudishness I had discovered his round hips, the harmonious curve of his shoulder. And, in that minute of abandon when he stretched, his towel at his fingertips and his bathing suit at his feet, I had also discovered the perfect form of that figure to which blood gave life. I knew that it was the same for Gerard, because we were almost the same—although he was a few months older, his eyes darker, and his hair lighter.

Gerard turned over on the grass. He had played the game, and the heat, beating against his temples, had put him to sleep. Of his face, I could see only the cheek. I stayed still. My blood stirred in my legs and in my arms, and I struggled not to put my head against his, not to hug him. Gerard slept. I watched in the broad daylight, my body leaning against his, troubled by the flesh that his unbuttoned shirt enveloped with a soft clarity while the sun whipped my shoulders with its invisible lash.

"Gerard, Gerard," I called him quietly, but he didn't hear. He was stolen from me by another life where, jealous of the embrace from which his body was excluded, he was perhaps watching me. "Gerard, Gerard," I pleaded.

The sound came from farther away than my throat. Was it the voice of the soul, this entreaty toward a being that I could no longer reach, and who would always hide himself in the labyrinth of sleep? An immense sadness took me in its arms. Everything seemed somber. Life was without meaning if Gerard could escape me so easily. How could this desert of sleep that belonged neither to death nor to existence, and whose sand also weighed heavy on my eyelids, come between us? Gerard's dull doze was already eternity.

Until this day, his simple existence was enough for me to ignore the fact that at seventeen years old, friendship is a name for love. For the first time, an unobtainable Gerard incapacitated me. Without thinking, I tore up a blade of rye grass. Leaving my melancholia next to my cousin, I turned toward the closest riverbank, parted the branches, lay down, and dunked the plant up to my fingertips. The grass blade disappeared after creating a ripple, but the wave it made did not reflect either my hand or my mouth leaning above it. On the river's edge I could make out only the green-gray shadow that was the reflection of the trees. Occasionally, like a stone thrown from the bank, a burst of sunlight fell right in the middle of the shadow that either delivered a band of river to its gigantic insurrection by moving a leaf, or else turned a piece of bark that lazed upon the still water into a luminous boat by lowering it imperceptibly toward the horizon.

I had to pick another stem, having abandoned mine to the gentle current next to the bank. I let go of that one as well, as if no longer sure that it wasn't in fact my desires that I was abandoning. This game fascinated me: the relaxation of a young Narcissus whose face the water didn't want to reflect. The blade of grass sunk and disappeared, so I began again. I picked another stem, and then another, so as to force myself not to look behind me at the defenseless body of my cousin. Suddenly something in me snapped—was it pride? I turned toward Gerard and brushed his hair with the rye. An interior voice whispered to me, "Take him in your arms." He groaned in his sleep, blindly spread his arms, and, without knowing what he was doing, pulled me toward him. He made me fall and held me with all his might. A pout deformed his lips. I was on top of him, but not breathing. His heat, his breath, became my own. The mystery of a body that one holds in his arms appeared both simple and terrible to me: to whom did he belong? The sleep distancing him from the Earth already took him to unknown regions. His somnolent isolation seemed like a glimpse of death.

I thought that by hugging me, Gerard was taking revenge for the water that I had splashed on him. I tried to free myself, saying,

"Gerard, let go." After a minute, however, I was fairly sure that he wasn't pretending to be asleep.

The sun painted his face with gold, magnifying his eyelids where the lashes had no shade, powdering his uncombed hair, fringing his ear with a transparent pink and putting little pearls of sweat about his inverted victim's neck. In just a second, he would turn over and stretch. I had only a moment to glimpse his defenselessness. Gerard's sleeping body had a nocturnal immensity. I put my ear to his heart. From so close, his mouth became that of an oracle. I would have done just about anything in order to hear the word *love* pronounced there.

He was still hugging me when he opened his eyes. Before wakefulness had given him back his memory, I caught a glance of a smiling face that I hadn't yet seen. To most people, my cousin had a dreamy, almost sly, look. His charm overwhelmed you almost as soon as you'd seen him. I, however, knew the real Gerard. I often grabbed his head when we wrestled and, tipping it into the sunlight, forced him to show me his eyes. They were flecked with green and brown, almost golden. I always let him go quickly to avoid losing myself in them.

One morning, we were fighting about a book that he swore he had loaned me. I suspected that he had actually left it in the barn where he liked to spend time alone, and where I had surprised him more than once, fire in his cheeks like someone emerging from a carnal dream. A wrestling match inevitably followed. Since he never triumphed when he let himself be overcome with anger, I soon strangled him between my legs, sat on his chest, and asked him if he gave up. Hate sparkled in his eyes. "No," he panted. "I'll squeeze, then," and with the same calm with which I said this, I took his wrist and twisted it. His forehead turned scarlet. I touched his burning cheek and casually brushed away the curls that fell into his eyes. He closed them. I commanded him to look at me, strengthening my hold on him. All of a sudden, as if to steal my face from me, he looked at me hard, his eyes full of tears. I let go. He didn't move. His face became serious, his pupils completely black, immense. His lashes, eyebrows, and hair scintillated with a thick sweat. A secret softness in his cheek and around his mouth seemed almost to beg me to hit them. Pain had revealed his tenderness to me, flashing over his features like the memory of his mother. I got up, but he remained on the ground. The last vision that I had before leaving was that of this tanned boy, one leg stretched tensely across the carpet, while the other, upright, communicated through the interplay of muscles barely discernable under his radiant skin an attitude of insolence in his humiliated pose.

I would have given up all the games, the provocations, the awkward desires that cut the day up into unforgettable moments, to get Gerard to reveal his true self to me. But he lied to me as he did to others. If this was the way he protected himself from people, then against which part of me was he defending himself? Was he afraid of losing the tyranny of his beautiful face? Didn't he know that a deeper charm would have united us? Through deliberate fits of bad temper, he quashed his most natural desires, like kissing me on the cheek to greet me each morning. He was afraid of his feelings, of tenderness . . .

In smiling at me, he had that look that I desired to see in him. I felt my blood drain from me as if I had been stabbed in the heart. We stared at each other in silence, our breaths short and shallow, our blood pulsing in our temples. I must have been beautiful myself, because Gerard was contemplating me, his jaw slack.

What a strange interior battle! I was fighting against myself. Half of me was Gerard; the other half pushed him away. It was a delicious but torturous moment. I already imagined our return: Gerard walking before me with his head down, in the rage of an afternoon where we hadn't managed to overcome our pride. Then, spurred on by my racing blood, I bent over the face that I loved. I broke through the hot screen of his breath, and with half-opened lips I felt his mouth open. Awkward and feverish, we didn't dare move. His small face gazed up at me. For me, Gerard transformed himself into two massive lips that I kissed. Numerous times we lost our breath and then recovered it by breathing the same air, without even pulling apart. Never had my heart been larger, and never had joy seemed so close to physical pain. My face kissed so much that it seemed to be made of ten thousand mouths. We were transformed. The past no longer existed. Our friendship took off its war mask and, slowly, love was going to put its hands on our new faces and gouge out our old hostile eyes. How long did we stay like that, our lips glued together, embracing so tightly that the smallest gesture would have hurt us? I don't know, but it must have been hours. And when, unable to bear it any longer, I thought I was in another world, I once again felt Gerard's tongue looking for mine. I discovered the veritable palace of his palette, which I explored with the wonderment of a child. Then I gave him my mouth, and in the fog of my first desire, I rolled to his side. We kissed each other with the violence of gladiators fighting for their lives. I reigned over his mouth as if it were the only place to which I could pay homage to our love. Gerard's saliva was as fresh as water, but his kiss made it burning hot. In a voice so quiet that I had to make him repeat it, he said, "You are beautiful." My look told him how much I admired him: these were our only declarations of love.

Suddenly, everything was different, yet nothing had changed. The summer day was no longer just a day of vacation spent next to the river, but the first day of the world. We were trapped, but still free to run as in the past. Now, to be ten steps apart would be like leaving each other. The first movement of love abolishes time, abolishes dreams, words, and insurrections against the person you love. It does not, however, abolish space. Space exists, more absolute than ever. The slow parade of sorrows and happy moments are necessary so that they, unfolding their long procession across the woods, fields, and rivers among which they lived, become connections for lovers. We detached our lips only to look each other in the eyes, our faces just a mouth's distance apart. Love was this marvelous garden whose gate we had at last dared to open to pick the flowers of the flesh.

I put my cheek on Gerard's. I saw the trees from their shady side, the landscape at once somber and sparkling. Between two bushes the entire plane stretched beyond the Loire. I saw small copses of trees and immense fields of wheat. The naked earth peeked between the parallel lines of vines that rose to meet the distance. The summer shone. There were little village houses, lost in the woods, whose windows gleamed. The purplish-blue of their roof tiles got mixed up with the vines and the plum trees. It was the light of love.

A violent tenderness made my whole body sensitive. Gerard's cheek was hot under mine. I touched the other side of his face with my hand, my palm caressing its curves. Despite a voluptuous cleft near the bottom of his chin, I could already discern the virile outline of his adult features. It was as if he was indignant to offer an adolescent's face up to life.

Gerard let go in order to stretch. Then, drawing me toward him, he licked my ear with a gentleness that weakened my courage. I closed my eyes. I had in me a whole landscape that we alone could see. The water, reflecting unreal trees, seemed gilded. Against the backlit valley, the woods unfolded their illusion. I wasn't on the grass anymore. There was no Loire, no horizons, no bluish fields, no vines. The only living thing was this brown boy whose fruity odor deviously invaded me. His shirt open on his golden skin and his T-shirt rolled beneath his head were the evidence of a miracle in which I believed. These everyday clothes became the instruments of adoration that made them no less than the lyre, the aegis, or the winged heels of the gods. We were at the age where symbols had direct meaning in our lives. I brought Gerard's hand to my mouth and crushed my face into his palm. He spread his fingers and gently squeezed. My lips, which pushed against the hollow of his palm in the middle of the lines of chance and life, wanted to inscribe their kiss there. I got up abruptly. Somehow, we were aware that we had just experienced the most beautiful day of our whole summer. We knew that it was more or less the end, since the sun was turning the color of pale blood. We moved with an astonishing slowness, so as not to miss any part of the day. Gerard, still half-lying on the ground, encircled my knees and pressed his big lips against them. Time ran around us.

Night was now falling; the curve of the horizon shone in the dusky sky. We had dinner every evening at eight o' clock. We hadn't realized how late it was, and were doubtlessly going to get in trouble at home. We started back passionlessly. Walking unconsciously, we left behind us the shadows of two boys at their first lovers' tryst.

When we opened the garden gate, my father was standing there. Without giving me any time to protect myself, he slapped me so hard that it knocked me backward. Gerard was next. They had apparently been waiting for us for a while. After this greeting, we continued across the yard in silence.

The house was illuminated, and lots of people were there. To the amusement of a few well-behaved teenagers whose parents pretended not to see us, my father threw us up the stairs and locked each of us in our rooms, upsetting everything as he went by: records, books, even the dart game he came across. I tried to turn on the light. The electrical fuses on the floor had been removed. How was I to get back to Gerard? They were having a good time below. I was hungry. An empty room separated our bedrooms. I grabbed a dictionary and looked up Morse code, but I would have had to tap too loudly in order to communicate. I tried some keys that I had presciently stolen from an armoire. None of them opened the door.

Steps in the hallway preceded my uncle. He tried a paternal tone: "What did you do this afternoon?" This was followed with some unpleasant suppositions. I kept silent.

"It's just a simple question.... So, you don't have anything to say? Well, since it's like that, we'll see you tomorrow at noon. Fasting and silence will be good counsel for you both. We're going to the Decazes' house for a murder-mystery party. Good night." He whistled as he shut the door.

Something had to be done. At that moment a small noise drew me to the window. I opened it. Gerard had pressed himself against the wall to make his way across the eight meters separating our windows on the narrow cornice that ran the perimeter of the house. He could have slipped and fallen to his death a million times.

He jumped into my arms: "My father came. We'll be alone until noon." We stayed quiet for a moment, listening for noises. Then the cars left, and we could hear the movement of our hearts. They beat quickly. This night would be a night of love.

II

I woke up, and shut my eyes again immediately, dazzled by the brightness of day. I turned over, and touched the body next to mine. Then I remembered everything, and pressed myself tenderly against Gerard's shoulder. He was sleeping on his stomach, his head turned toward me, his lips parted by his shallow breath. His hair was tousled, his body uncovered to the waist, and he had only one leg under the red blanket. The hot night had partially undressed us in such a way that we were half on a wrinkled sheet and half on the blood-red fabric held under one of Gerard's legs. The other leg shined a dull metallic yellow. I could follow the black line of his body, from his ankle to his armpit, which his breath made tremble slightly. I gently pulled away the fabric that was rolled around one thigh in order to have that statue of a sleeping boy entirely before my eyes. It was as if Gerard was emerging from the crimson; the same somber shine of blood was in the splendid color of his flesh.

A delicious fatigue crushed every part of my body, the base of my neck above all. We gave ourselves to each other until our exhausted forces left us defenseless. In one night we wanted to know all of love's secrets. Rage presided over this discovery, to the moment that dawn revealed two young male lovers in sated but unfulfilled bodies.

I put my hand on his back where a small mouth of sun bit into his flesh as it infiltrated the room through the gaps in the blinds. It wanted to know the next episode of our story. I was so exhausted that I drifted off once again. Gerard's movements woke me for good. Night left his eyes. He felt my lassitude. His head and legs were slack. We were stretched out next to each other, seemingly without any strength, although our youth demanded a triumphant dawn . . .

The bedroom was besieged by the day. Long arrows of sunlight shot into the wall, the ground, and the bed where they pierced our bodies and made them one. We stayed still for a while after our pleasure; I embraced Gerard and slowly stroked his skin. I imagined myself on an adventure in the ocean of the sky. The bed was my boat. This beautiful naked boy asleep next to me would make me capsize. He tossed ceaselessly, his thigh brushing against my palm. My hand couldn't exhaust the softness of this skin resisting my flesh. This skin that actually longed for the grip, or rather the bite, or even the blow that would break the proud beauty of a body that possessed all forms of desire, of touch, and of sight. Even the ultimate possession—entering his body—didn't mean anything except the impossibility of being him. I didn't want just to penetrate him. I wanted to devour him, to seize him, to be in his skin without changing one bit of our infinite caresses. We stayed silent. The simple touch of his shoulder gave me an erection. I put my mouth to his ear; the hairs at the nape of his neck caressed my cheek. My hand descended the length of his back. My blood stopped. It seemed as if I touched a different body each time. Vanquished by his lascivious nature, he took the pillow in his arms and gave himself up. Not an inch of his body was forbidden to me.

Under the appearances of this vigorous boy, life had thus marked the path of my future. Good-bye to the lycées where I was learning to become like the others; this artificial culture of success revolted me. I wanted to be free, free to love a body like my own. I built a crystal fortress around our life, well aware that others would try to break it. I sensed ahead of time my cousin's refusal, his lies crumbling like a house of cards with his father's first appeal to his virile pride. Death was watching him to see if he would take adult games as seriously as he did his childhood amusements. I remembered one of the first scenes when we really became friends; it was in Paris, freshman year, at Lycée Carnot. We were fifteen. No one liked Gerard; he didn't have any friends because he acted snobby and pretended to be bored by everyone. He was also known as someone who loved to fight dirty. Even if he was losing, he dealt blows that hurt as much to give as to receive.

He didn't deign to take part in schoolyard brawls, but instead refused authority in his own way. When he slept under the nose of the professors, for example, they showed him a guilty indulgence. Only one teacher, the one in charge of students studying Greek and Latin, had chosen him as his favorite prey. We called him "Oum-oum" among ourselves. He was a very young man, with a long thin face that we found beautiful, and who displayed a Machiavellian irony toward Gerard. He was always quizzing him on the rules of syntax, making him get up in front of the silent class in order to make fun of the poetic style of his essays and to overwhelm him with the help of Cicero and Catullus.

Gerard resisted pouting impassively, and lifted his head proudly when laughter greeted a particularly well-aimed arrow. He was completely indifferent toward work. When the professors showed him, in front of the whole class, that they considered him charming (but above all good at Ping-Pong or tennis following several exciting matches where people saw him taking previously uncontested champions out of action), Gerard then astonished them with one of his unusually good essays, products of his juvenile fervor and solitary nature. Oum-oum, mortally wounded by this particularly successful Tacitus, would not pardon him.

Like all fifteen-year-old boys, we had created a kingdom defended by Spartan law to which we submitted ourselves wholeheartedly. We had a code, rites, and rights. There existed a secret counsel whose purpose was to fight seditious projects and whose maneuvers tended toward absolutism. The seven of us represented a small welfare committee that reigned terror on the playground and in the schoolyard. Our thugs were charged with inventing torments for people in other gangs in order to distract us during our free time and to satisfy our innate cruelty. Our pleasure was exacted in a thousand different ways. Alternately, we brought into fashion the romanticism of Scottish vests, walking sticks, long hair, and then à la Titus, swearing like sailors. We wore silver bracelets on our wrists, and like soldiers, we commemorated the exploits of our club by notching them.

Gerard lived outside of these rules. Although a silent hostility existed against him and his insolence, our fraternity tolerated him since the group wanted me to be one of the leaders of our clan.

Before classes we met on Malherbes Boulevard. We arrived in small groups. When I reached the lycée's sidewalk, I abandoned Gerard and his loner attitude. It was here that we organized boycotts while running after girls and exchanging math homework. We had unanimously decided several days prior to create an infernal scene that afternoon. The unexpected absence of the precept being an immense help, we entered the lycée in an overexcited state. Only Gerard did not know what was going on, or rather pretended that he didn't. As I caught up with the members of the gang, they grilled me:

"And monsieur, your cousin. . . . What's he doing?"

"Nothing," I answered.

"Okay then, let's get him in on it."

I approached Gerard and told him of an alarm clock under the podium, of the acid with which "Oum-oum's" drawer was full. I described for him the Latin assignments (none of which was completed as prescribed, but which were instead illustrated like comic books), the spoken chorus that we had prepared for Esther's stanzas, and the demonic cries that would noisily cover the professor's attempt to open a carefully locked door after his entry into our lair.

Gerard shrugged his shoulders. "My compliments for what will surely be an award-winning performance," he said sarcastically.

I admitted rhyming the choruses and bringing the alarm clock. He became quieter; I foresaw a drama. Rebuffed by Oum-oum, Gerard applied himself *sans juxta* to translating his Latin homework, which lent him a troubling beauty during class. He lowered his head. A boy pushed him: "We're sick of you acting like a coward. You and your beautiful face will get what they deserve!" The Rubicon had been crossed.

The class began in a chilly atmosphere. Little by little, various noises began to disturb the voice of the person reading aloud the orators of the constituency. Oum-oum became irritated, and with a dry thwack, smacked his ruler against the edge of the desk. A violent burst of laughter erupted, and was immediately stifled; the ruler, which had been adroitly scored, was in pieces. A heavy silence glued us to our chairs. Oum-oum gave us the look of a lion tamer who knew that he was about to be devoured. Then, the alarm clock rang, and the voice of a captive rose above the murmur to recite the marvelously scanned chorus:

> *Pleurs et gémissions, mes compagnons fidèles,*
> *Aux pleurs amers donnons un libre cours,*
> *A nos efforts les Latins sont rebelles:*
> *Tuons-les tous et sans autre discours . . .*
>
> (Cry and moan, my faithful companions,
> To our bitter cries, let's give free reign,
> Against our efforts, the Romans rebel,
> Let's kill them, without further delay . . .)

Voices joined in one after another. We were thirty against one. Oum-oum had been laid low by the blow, and was slowly recuperating. We were waiting for him to get up, and to run among us. We had foreseen this, and thus had reinforcements, in case one of us found himself cornered. After that, there would be a rush for the door, but we had checked the hinges, which would last at least until our final chorus. The show had to last until the final scene featuring Oum-oum, vanquisher of door locks!

Inexplicably Gerard turned, and grabbed the paper from the hands of a stupid kid who was using it to remember his two stanzas. Oum-oum was waiting for a sign: he had it, and in two bounds was on top of my cousin, whom he took by the collar and dragged to the podium. The class stopped breathing. Gerard's gesture was his admission of innocence, and a word from him would have been enough to ruin everything: he resorted to his usual, obstinate silence. Oum-oum hovered over Gerard as if he were a beast of prey, and then, as if the boy didn't exist, he righted the desk, put the alarm clock on it, and said in a flat voice: "To whom does this instrument belong?"

No one had time to open his mouth. Everything happened as quickly as the crack of a whip. Gerard answered: "The alarm clock is mine, sir." Oum-oum, tragically furious, slapped Gerard so hard that he fell on his knees at the foot of the podium.

I admired him; it was one of those silent scenes that mark people for life. He got up, but Oum-oum had resolved to teach him a lesson. Seizing the right triangle that hung from a nail to the right of the blackboard, he beat his buttocks, his thighs, and his back all the way to his shoulders. Moved, we listened to the breath that spurted from his mouth like a sigh ripped from his whole body by the beauty of this boy. Gerard balled his fists and bit his lips. I counted fifteen blows, but there were probably more.

    A little later, after Gerard was back at his seat, we reopened our books. A morose intoxication kept us in that room where the emptiness of the blackboard was still inscribed with the image of the raised arm of a man who had beaten a boy with blows that seemed like the silent screams of our hearts.

    Class ended and we had chemistry next. When we finally left school, the autumn wind blew the dead leaves about. I caught up with my faction outside the building. Gerard hadn't come out yet. Christian, the boy who had treated him like a coward earlier that afternoon, said to me: "We'll get him later this evening; we're all for it, and you'd better be, too!" There wasn't anything else to do but wait. My cousin appeared with a couple of students and crossed the playground. Christian blocked his way, his hands in his pockets. Gerard understood, backed up a few steps, and stood with his back against a metal post, in the middle of the circle that was slowly closing in on him. He didn't say a word. He was ready to fight. On every side, there were faces whose passion was hidden by the twilight.

    Michel, one of our seven, audaciously told him what we were going to do to him: we had indelible ink that we were going to use to draw a Maltese cross, which was our insignia, on his ass. Then we were going to use a whip to drive it into the skin. Gerard rolled up his raincoat and put it and his book bag against the pillar. A boy grabbed his forearm, but a swift punch made him let go. There was a moment's pause. The wind, the dust, and the barely lighted playground were the violet color of the skin next to a wound. All of a sudden two boys threw themselves on Gerard, heads down, not worrying about his fists, and immobilized him against the post. Two others grabbed his knees. Maurice, a young demon with a boxer's nose, opened Gerard's jacket, ripped off his school tie, and exposed, in the pale light of his unbuttoned shirt, the ruddy torso of my cousin. Gerard tried to fight in vain. Large drops of sweat made his hair stick to his temples, shining. Maurice undid his belt.

Gerard closed his eyes and let it happen. I was the only one to see a tear run down his cheek. Forcefully I cried, "Stop! Let only one person fight him. If Gerard wins, he can go free." Fighting even a battered and bruised Gerard made them hesitate. Christian suggested insidiously, "Well, then, go ahead." I gave Gerard the time to take off his jacket and to button up his shirt. He thought I wanted to humiliate him as they did. He gathered his strength so that I'd have to call on all of mine. Or perhaps it was so that he'd lose consciousness once he became the prey of these boys, who, without shame, would throw themselves upon him while pinning his shoulders to the ground. We threw ourselves on each other and rolled about on the pavement. Gerard was crushing my neck when I realized that his knees and back were hurting, undoubtedly a result of that afternoon's beating. I grabbed him around the waist to prove to him that I could defeat him. We were face to face and the wind filled our open mouths with dust and debris.

His grip loosened bit by bit. With a jerk, as if to free myself, I flipped us over and glued my back to the ground. I could hear his heart through his torn shirt; an odor of triumph rose from his armpit. We got up. He picked up his things and left without a word.

When we were on the boulevard, a boy from the group spoke up. "It's better that someone from his family beat him up; he's a tough one!" My reputation risked being damaged, but I was happy to have helped Gerard. When I went home, there were only four places set. Gerard had used a headache as a pretext to go to bed right away. I didn't dare go upstairs, although he was all I could think about. I imagined him in a sheet-bound hell. The meal was gloomy. I was continually distracted by questions to which I gave only monosyllabic answers. In my head I ceaselessly reconstructed images that I was being forced to abandon. Trying not to leave the table too quickly, at last I opened Gerard's door. He was on his knees next to the bed, one hand spread out on the sheets, the other against his body. On the leg nearest to me, he'd pulled up his woolen sock. A brown spot of dried blood stuck it to his skin.

The other leg was bare, except for the scratches and their dried blood. It might seem surprising, but happily I was the first one to see them. He had taken off his jacket. Between his pants and his shirt, which was halfway off his back, his lower back glistened. His dark skin evoked profound desires in me. I already imagined him surrounded by prairies and woods where we would be able to be naked. Sadness made me feel all choked up.

His eyes were closed. In the lamplight, tears still trembled on his lashes. I shook his shoulder, but he didn't move. I took him in my arms and hoisted him onto the bed. The place where his face had been was moist. Over this secret pain, fatigue had won out. I didn't really think that I'd saved him, however, or that he loved me.

The next day was Thursday. Gerard didn't seem to remember anything that had taken place yesterday evening. He just wore a jersey over his shirt for a few days under the pretext that winter was approaching, and smiled at me clandestinely a few times . . .

Later that night, I touched and retouched his upper back, divided by that line that makes backs look like fruit sometimes. Gerard stopped my hand at the base of his hair. I felt my cousin's heart beating against my palm through his trembling nape. The barriers of physical pride having been broken, another more secret barricade went up between us. It let sighs out, voluptuous murmurs, even cries of pleasure, but stopped cries of love. Since last evening, we'd taken a thousand steps toward each other, but a thousand still separated us. Neither one of us wanted to make the next move.

Gerard got up. Once again I found in his hot breath a whole night lost in the desire to annihilate ourselves. We didn't realize that love needs two bodies, not to melt them into each other, but to throw them together, each person desiring to extract the prize of his love from the other. Were we like anyone else? In loving him, I hadn't stopped saying his first name silently to myself. I'm sure he was saying mine, as well. What we were waiting for was still unpronounceable, however.

He clenched his teeth while kissing in order to delay the offering of his mouth. This was amusing and irritating at the same time. I held his lips between my fingers; their arc opened a little and from this cup I drank the wine of giddiness. From one instant to another, the day filtered lighter and lighter into the bedroom. We got up. The rays of sun through the blinds and the trees threw spotted shadows on us so that we looked liked leopards. Gerard stretched. His suppleness and his face, which the morning made into an animal's muzzle, augmented his feline appearance. The sensual odor of the night that prowled about the room seemed to emanate from his skin.

I pushed the shutters back. A flood of light inundated the walls and the furniture, the bed. The red of the blanket became more intense, the sheets more wrinkled. The flow of air chased away the nocturnal scents that strayed in the corners. We were naked and bathed in sunlight. Gerard squinted in order to see me, because the sun was behind my body, which was surrounded by a halo of sunlight. He offered me his chest, which his breath raised with the gentleness of a lover's hand. My kisses landed on his giggling mouth.

Then we made up the bed. We had rediscovered nudity and original sin. It was the hour that forced us to slip into our clothes, but the charm was not destroyed. A violent intimacy made words useless. Each of Gerard's gestures sent me into a new country in which Gerard alone would satisfy me, and from which I would never return.

By my watch it was eight o' clock. The cousin who was taking care of us always got up late. The others had most certainly not yet come back, since the house was still. As a precaution, we agreed that Gerard should go back to his room. I took him in my arms for a good-bye that we would have to endure for several hours. We were so happy that we were afraid of even this short absence. Even this brief separation showed us that the time we had enjoyed together was in reality just a temporary clearing of the sky before the impending storm and the total eclipse of the sun.

As if his room were the destination of a long trip, I kissed his eyes, his forehead, and then his ears. He put his lips on my cheeks and pressed so hard that their impression remained there an instant. Twice he was on the verge of climbing out the window; twice he came back to take me in his arms and to lift my head to fix my features in his memory. At last, tearing himself regretfully from our love, I saw him cross the border, filling the room with his shadow for an instant. Then, like a supernatural boy, he disappeared into the daylight.

I remained where I was for a long while. I already wanted to go back to Gerard. Each second intensified this desire to the verge of folly. Thus, our fragile human existence deprived me of my cousin, like the conjurer who makes an illusion out of an illusion. A few minutes were enough to kill a too-beautiful night—even fewer would have sufficed for Gerard and my youth to follow the same path. At that age where everything takes on fateful proportions, we were brusquely forced to face one evening of our destiny. I remembered the silence of my father after the death of his wife. His sadness was not the same as mine, even though she had been my mother. Gerard had known the same feelings of alienation. Our fathers, not very close before their respective grieving, decided to simplify their lives and to remember the happiness of their youth. Their businesses completed their connection so it was natural for us to all live together, with few thoughts about our desires or our arrogant pride. My father had told me of their decision one evening upon my return from school. The next day, a cousin came to get me at the end of class, since the furniture was being moved the next morning. He was sure that my cousin Gerard and the big yard behind our new house on Malherbes Boulevard would make me very happy.

On moving day, I played hooky, and shut myself in an already empty room. I sat in the darkness, listening to the tumult of the movers to which the echoes of the violated house responded. It was as if a storm had let loose in the apartment whose sudden rage had turned the furniture into dangerous reefs in the calm sea of the day. I looked at the street through the blinds. A young workman in blue overalls was taking my books to the truck. He had full lips. The young sun of February nibbled at his arms. From his undershirt rose a round neck on which a vein popped with effort. A lock of hair fell on his forehead, which he now and again brushed out of the way by throwing his head back. The bottoms of his pants were rolled halfway up his calves. Above the socks that were rolled around his ankles, his ivory skin revealed calves that I would have liked to caress. I stayed there all morning watching his comings and goings, pushed toward his beauty, desiring a smile from that blond workman whom I imagined to be available for kisses. When he finally entered my room, all I got was a "Get out of here, kid . . ."

At five o'clock, my female cousin was waiting for me at the entrance to the school. Even though I had arrived there only minutes before, I made as though I was just leaving it. She took me to the new house on Malherbes Boulevard. There was a large hallway from which a staircase ascended. My father and my uncle were in the living room, in the middle of the furniture, the books, and the rolled carpets. It was there that I discovered Gerard, to whom I'd barely paid attention in the past because he had never been particularly popular. He stood a bit apart, near the window, his head inclined, studying the boy coming toward him with his hand extended. He shook it gravely, and then proposed that we explore the attic together, which was to be our bedroom. It was made of two large, low rooms—one for each of us—that were separated by an opening whose door had been removed.

Gerard had already created chaos in his room. He looked at me without saying a word while I put my stuff away. After dinner, my cousin sprawled in an armchair, observing my movements with the same silence. My heart swelled. I was on the verge of desperation, and, getting hold of myself, I almost shouted to him, "I feel like sleeping. I'm going to bed." He got up, turned, and went to his room. I got undressed. Once in bed, I had forgotten to put the light out. I was going to get up when Gerard, in pajamas, went toward the lamp and made a movement that meant, "Do you want me to turn it off?" Darkness invaded the bedroom. I was dazzled as thousands of lights still sparkled beneath my lids. An instant later the scissors of the moon sliced through the diamond-shaped window at the roof's peak. Gerard approached, took my head in his hands, and kissed my cheek with childlike maternal tenderness. He had adopted me; happiness put me to sleep.

From this day on a clandestine fight began between us. We wanted to ignore each other, but there was this first night between us. Now another night had just negated our lovers' blindness and had reduced our seventeen-year-olds' pride to make us break our silence and kneel before each other, like vassals making a vow. The universe, the night, the sun, the Earth, the stars might pass, but not love. For me, love had golden-brown hair, a full mouth, and the melancholy violence of a lover. Gerard was my life. We could give in to bodily caprice: we were innocent.

III

We were kept in lockdown for a whole day, and then the surveillance let up. After all, we were on vacation. Any old excuse was now enough for us to get away from them. We wanted to be alone. Everything about each other remained to be discovered: the body's caprices, the other's desires. Gerard was on the point of knowing more than me, but he had to see right away that I kept no holds barred with him.

He had always liked a huge old barn where I suspected him of jerking off sometimes. I followed him there now. In the violent shadows of the morning sunlight, he took off his clothes and threw himself on a tarp covering a bed of hay. On his brown skin, I could make out two slightly darker shadows. The one below his forehead was the pit of his eyes; the other, below his stomach, attracted me.

Destiny needs time to play itself out! It makes two boys go along on the same path for days, months, and then suddenly it chooses its dusk and allows them to meet up and to take each other in their arms. I was wise beyond my years, like all seventeen-year-old boys. I wanted to rediscover our first memory in common, to redo just one gesture differently because, with each image of the past, it would have taken almost nothing to change our love. This was just a dream; only the present mattered. What good would it have been to discover more quickly that we loved each other if our hearts just wanted to fool themselves? We needed these troubling moments, the unspoken desires. The solitary pleasures when thinking of the other and the fights that we didn't understand could turn the first kiss near the pond into the first kiss in the whole world. The past gave us the gift of blind memory. This would serve us, because everything would try to separate us: habits, conventions, the rules of life. Something stronger was needed to slice through the Gordian knot of our passion, since that was what it was now: a passion. Despite the thirteen years we had known each other, little by little we had become strangers to each other as we were growing up—that is, until the night where, having become adolescents, we two children looked at each other for the first time, and, under the low blows of love, remained defenseless . . .

It was night. We were in our rooms, preparing for the baccalaureate exam. I was finishing an algebra problem. Gerard was supposed to be finishing an essay, but was instead taking advantage of his Latin dictionary's giant margins to draw the legs and heads of Roman warriors. Not hearing him move, I called to him, "How's it going, Gerard? Are you working?" A groan that I took for a "yes" arose from the other room. I solved the equation and, without putting anything away, got up. A feeling of strength ran through me. I wasn't a child anymore. I was aware of my whole body; my clothes were caressing my skin. I perceived the smallest friction. In my chest beat a torrent whose impetuous course took life all the way to the ends of my fingertips. My body was a beast that wanted to devour my heart. I didn't see things the same way anymore: the leather bindings of the books looked like skin, the wood of the furniture like a trembling forest; colors had a taste. Every step revealed to me the force of my leg muscles. A deep breath made my shirt come alive. I felt proud, like a heroic statue, and, although I don't know why, indefinably unhappy.

For a little while now, people had been staring at me in the street. Coming back alone from the lycée, I had decided to hang about in Monceau Park until night fell. There was a group of students seated next to the fake ruins of the temple of love, their notebooks and textbooks on a chair. The path narrowed here. They stopped talking when I passed near them. I had barely gone by when I heard one of them say aloud, "That guy is handsome!" I blushed and remembered that scene.

In the evenings, which sparkled colorlessly like a diamond, I could just see the dark roofs and trees of Paris. Sensing Gerard's presence in his room threw me into the same troubled happiness. The sensual odor of linden trees, a smell of spring, invaded the room and made my head spin. I entered Gerard's room. Leaning over his book, he didn't hear me. His neck offered itself to me in the semidarkness. I became furious: "You're still fooling around, blowing off your homework?

That's really wrong! You have no willpower." Gerard didn't move. I continued: "And you're such a liar!"

He pushed his chair back violently and said, "Shut up!" He came to the door between our rooms and stood there, glaring. He was in the shadows, ready to throw himself on me.

I took the most offhanded tone. "Nice look. You want me to give you a little kiss with my fist?"

Suddenly his voice became another body that stood between us in the room. It had become more heated and, despite the tone of what he said, aggressively sensual. "You're going to eat those words."

He moved toward me. I braced myself, but it was as if we were seeing each other for the first time. We were shocked because our clothing wasn't hiding our coiled fists, our shoulders, or our strong thighs any longer. Gerard's open collar revealed his ivory-white neck, strong, smooth, and sensual in a way that I suddenly desired very much. The smallest gesture and everything would topple over. We felt like idiots standing before each other, but neither of us had the courage to confront his beating heart. Then Gerard lowered his eyes, lightened the tone of his voice, and said that he was going to bed. He'd finish his essay tomorrow. He seemed, however, to hesitate. My hands felt like groping him, and my chest told me, "He will touch you, if you want." But I heard my voice, as if from far away, say "Good night," and then Gerard's retreating footsteps.

I got undressed furiously and slid naked between the sheets. They seized my body, stuck themselves to it. I needed this caress so as not to go running to my cousin. I listened to the sound of books being closed, the table being pushed back, shoes being taken off, pants sliding off his legs, his shirt being pulled over his head. He had to be naked now himself. The groan of the bed told me that he was in it. I could not sleep. A clock chimed, marking the hours one by one. They would have all seemed the same if it weren't for the deepening darkness and the increasingly profound silence. I didn't dare stir. I was in a furnace of sheets, my sweaty skin sticking to the cloth. Barely audible creaks told me that Gerard was also tossing and turning, but that he didn't dare budge from his bed, either. I knew that he was imagining himself in my arms as I was imagining myself in his. All it would have taken was for me to get up; in ten steps, I would have been next to him. My bed was, however, a stronghold of arrogant pride. I caressed Gerard by caressing my own body.

    Thanks to our final exams, we were able to avoid each other for a few days. Then came two weeks of vacation and the sleepiness of my cousin one summer day next to the water, which let our hearts hear each other once again.
    A bird sang in a tree next to the barn, which made the silence more deafening. Gerard looked at me cagily. He laughed: "You're serious this morning!" His voice killed that of the bird whose song had managed to reach us through the heavy door and through the bundles of hay on which we lay, whose thirst-making odor mixed with the smell of drying clover. I undressed and laid down next to Gerard. The hay scratched my shoulder and my calf as we moved, but his body became only softer and more caressing. The morning breathed its humid breath, its way of yawning, the caprices of its slumber, the haste of its heart. The closer noon got, the darker the barn became; between the door and the wall, one could make out a tree, and farther on, splotches of light, blindly brilliant like steel. We got dressed. Gerard wanted to stay, and begged: "Too bad for them. So they'll eat without us. Then they'll lock us in our rooms and I'll get out through the window and we'll be happy again . . ." It was absurd. He sprawled out in the hay again. I tried to get him up, but he pulled me down on top of him, kissed my whole face, unbuttoned his shirt and turned over on the cut hay; he was out of his mind. His chest brushed my cheek. My lips went from one nipple to the other. Gerard stopped my mouth on his left one, above his heart. He groaned while lifting himself up, a groan that I soon made into one of pain as I bit, my face buried in his torso. I would have liked to feed off this flesh. I took him by the nape of the neck and told him sternly to get dressed. We'd come back here later.
    In fact, we didn't return afterward because Gerard had to study during this vacation. He had failed the oral part of his baccalaureate. Everyone was expecting this, just as they were expecting my success, even though Gerard easily turned this failure into a triumph. He

couldn't give a damn about an exam that was nowadays the aspiration of every shopkeeper, according to him. This reasoning would have earned him a vacation in some provincial summer school if I hadn't sacrificed, less from generosity than from the fear of not seeing him, a trip to Corsica and my passion for underwater adventures in exchange for this house in Touraine, which friends loaned my father every summer. Gerard didn't thank me. He didn't regret anything, and he hadn't since Carnot—not the numerous lycées out of which his laziness got him kicked (forcing me to follow), not the sermons of my father, not even the punishments from his own. None of this bothered him a bit. He was capable of learning the stuff he'd ignored all trimester in just one day, thereby getting himself pardoned thanks to the fantastic grades and sardonic remarks with which his report card was covered.

In May, he had turned seventeen. That day, I was allowed to invite a few friends over to celebrate. Despite his reputation, his charm won them over and he became a god for the entire class—a dark god, of course, since a face like his, with its haughty and rebellious air, made people look at him during class. At the party, he put the finishing touches on his conquest by inventing some weird sort of Iroquois Indian dance, which he performed half-naked, his body streaked with red, white circles like bracelets on his legs and arms. He had even found multicolored strands of yarn that he wore around his ankles. Mouth-watering desire shone in the eyes of the boys. A few weeks later, it occurred to me that they had left our house hopelessly in love with him.

The first mornings of vacation were gloomy. I read while Gerard worked halfheartedly. He was dreaming of the magic word "vacation." I watched him sit there, his hand on his cheek, his eyes out to sea, hair blowing in the wind, a cry lodged in his throat. When he realized that I had followed him on his imaginary voyage, he picked up his book again and said meanly, "You're mad at me for having brought you here to this 'idyllic retreat.' Aren't you, Mr. Genius?"

When we fell in love with each other, Gerard changed. He decided to work and, for a few days, bravely stood up to his lazy nature. Then, thanks to me, he was defeated anew.

I wanted him to return to the barn, but as he hadn't done anything all morning, he put me off: "It's you who wants me to do this stuff." He told me, "Come help me or come read in my room."

I refused. He went upstairs alone, and I shouted to him, "Come find me when you've had enough."

Humming to myself, I left. When I got to the barn I could see the impression of our bodies in the hay. I went to lie down in the hollow that they had made.

I rolled around on an imaginary Gerard. An interior voice called to him, "I'm waiting for you. I want you to come." A minute passed. Gerard did not come. I asked someone, I'm not sure whom, "Make him come. If you're powerful, he'll be here right away."

A second elapsed. Gerard opened the door, ashamed at having given in. He stood there in the daylight. I kept silent. He thought that I disapproved, but didn't try to make any excuses. My attitude bothered him. He was full of indignation, his cheeks hot, his forehead flushed, his mouth wet. "Screw homework," he said, "I'm against what they're trying to make me learn, anyway. Youth should mean freedom. They're trying to get us to live our whole lives in captivity, until our skin becomes the color of the paper of our books. I won't do it! I won't!"

I answered with all the calmness in the world, "Gerard, take off your shirt. You're going to get hot."

He sat down near me. I touched his cheek. It was hot and soft. I touched his mouth, but before I had the time to hold him, he made off like a banshee toward the house.

Hours later, when I went back to my room, his door was closed and locked. I knocked. I begged. He wouldn't open it. I pressed my ear to the door, and heard him holding his breath. I left my post and went toward my room. A letter on the table surprised me. I opened it and read:

> *Pierre, my sweet Pierre. I've behaved badly. I'd promised you I'd study, but I was distracted by the desire to see you. From now on, I'll only tell you that I love you. I would like to be at your feet when you read this. Don't ever mention this letter to me. When you're not there,*

the world is with you. I live in a shadow and this shadow is love. I want you to love me.

Gerard

PS: I wrote you a poem. I was afraid you'd get back before I'd finished it. I didn't do any translating, since I worked on this all afternoon in my room.

This poem was written on another sheet, which was folded in half:

Tu es mon EXTASE

Ecarte-toi, l'amour est un briseur d'images!
Les rêves de ton corps explosent dans ma chair
Qu'espères-tu, ma nuit l'a déjà tout offert.
Mon cœur, ma peau, mon sang, mon sexe et mon visage.

Pourquoi m'attaches-tu? Je ne peux plus te fuir.
Si tu m'ouvrais les yeux, tu t'y verrais toi-même.
Ton cœur contre mon cœur, sans se dire qu'on s'aime.
Je veux entre tes bras mourir de trop jouir.

J'ai crié, tout éclate et mon âme ravie
Monte dans un abîme . . . Il faut prendre ma vie.
Tu me rends immortel quand tu crois me tuer.
Vien, je suis ton désert sans oasis ni terme,
Je rêve de t'y perdre et j'ai pour abreuver
Toutes tes soifs mon sang, ma salive et mon sperme.

(You are my ECSTASY

Stand back, love destroys all images!
Dreams of your body explode in my flesh.
What are you hoping for? My night has already offered you everything,
My heart, my skin, my blood, my dick, my face.
Why have you tied me up? I can no longer leave you.

If you opened my eyes, you'd see yourself,
Your heart against my heart, without saying, "I love you,"
I want to die in your arms of too much joy.

I cried out, everything exploded, and my ravished soul
Fell into an abyss . . . I must die.
You make me immortal by thinking that you're killing me.
Come! I am your boundless, oasis-less desert.
I dream that you'll lose yourself in me, and that I will slake
All your thirsts with my blood, my saliva and my sperm.)

My heart beating, I dashed out into the hall. My cousin's voice surged forward from the depths of me, climbing into my chest and putting all of his words of love into my mouth. Their violence intoxicated me. I knocked on his door. Everything was still, and yet I could tell he was close, on the other side of the door, his head pressed against the wood. I could have drawn the outline of his body, so strongly did I sense it pressed against the door that I vainly wanted him to open. He revealed himself with every exhalation. His breath was so close that his lips had to be on the door. I kissed the wall passionately, and threw myself against it. We were like two lovers separated by a prison wall, more visible to each other now than in the suffocation of their kisses, showing more love here than through their gestures of love.

I murmured quietly, my heart crushed by these mad feelings: "Gerard, are you angry? Answer me. Open the door just for a second, Gerard; open." Gerard threw himself against the door, banged it, and shook the handle. I calmed him. "Gerard, listen to me. What's wrong? Open the door!"

"I threw the key from the window as hard as I could. My father is outside. I can't crawl out the window," he answered.

With three bounds I was in the garden. Gerard appeared at his window, but couldn't help me. He only remembered throwing it as far as he could. By some miracle, I found the key against some edging that ran around the grass and help it up high, brandishing it against the sky. At that moment, my uncle came out across the veranda. I stopped, my hand aloft.

"What are you doing with that key?" he asked me. I was speechless: "I dropped it. It's the key to my room."

"You're locking your door now?"

"No, uncle, but . . ."

He imitated me mockingly, "No, uncle, but . . ." Gerard watched my antics from above. I took his interest for morbid curiosity. Speaking to Gerard, he said, "Why don't you explain it to me, stool pigeon?" Gerard blushed, but didn't move. My uncle got irritated. "Do you want me to come upstairs?"

I interrupted him, "Uncle, I locked Gerard in his room and was teasing him from here. He didn't do anything, but he couldn't get out."

That got him going. "Excellent, my boy. Well, then, I'll just keep the key and he can work until dinner. Now, scram!"

I went back upstairs, kneeled before Gerard's door, and kissed it with all my might.

Back in my room, I hid the letter and the poem that had been lying on the table, angry with myself for having left them at the mercy of my uncle, who could have gone upstairs to see if I was lying or why I was locking my door. My heart needed Gerard more and more. If one of his smiles could make me feel alive, then his unhappiness made me sad—not in the indecisive melancholy way of adolescents, but with the kind of sadness reserved for someone you love. The kind that impulsively passes from joy to overwhelming despair, from hopelessness to malice.

I waited for the evening meal, my forehead pressed against the window. The trees of the park glowed in the sun, their bark dried by a red fire that darkened with the day, making them look so much like towers of ash that it seemed as though the lightest breath would turn them into dust and scatter them across the grass. I wished that everything was like that, and that all it would have taken to get rid of everything was my desire. The countryside, the park, my bedroom would all disappear, and a new existence with Gerard would begin before my astonished eyes. His father's actions had erected an insurmountable barrier between Gerard and his studies. This is what he told me, in an insolent manner when, after dessert, we left the adults to their coffee and their bridge game. It was still light out. My cousin took me toward the kitchen garden.

Gardening was his father's pastime. Each morning he came to admire his lettuce lovingly, which stood proudly in its raffia corsets, and to fondle his melons, which were waking up under their glass bells like self-satisfied bankers disturbed by the cock's crow. He swooned over his thyme and chervil, and beamed at his espaliers of apples and pears. He stayed there every day until noon at least, his head covered by a straw hat and his hoe in his hand. He was protecting his progeny, watching out for weeds and insects, putting mulch here, removing a windbreak there. He was there so often and cared so much for his plants that it wouldn't have surprised us if he had taken root there and started to sprout leaves.

Gerard took a slingshot out of his pocket, calmly picked up a pebble from the walk, aimed, and destroyed the first glass bell. The air filled with the sound of shattering crystal. I didn't protest; I was overcome. One after the other, each glass cover was broken. More than one, struck exactly in the middle, exploded like a landmine. I asked Gerard to leave the last one for me. He handed me his slingshot. I watched my stone hit the glass and reduce it to shards. Gerard grabbed me around the waist, trembling, his mouth humid with saliva, his fingers filled with earth.

Before us, the neat furrows were gone; it looked like a bomb had been dropped. Gerard wanted some sort of an apotheosis. He unscrewed a watering pipe, splashed about, and then opened the valves of the cistern. Rainwater spewed out in torrents, drowning the seedlings, carrying the glass debris across the garden. A miniature tulip planted between the red currant bushes and the tool shed started to drown. Gerard's shirt, covered with spray and wet to the shoulder, stuck to his flesh. Its transparency revealed his skin. Getting up, he burst out laughing: "And that's not all, citizen!" he said to me. "On to the Bastille!" The Bastille was what we called the Decazes' pigeon house. We had to cross two vegetable gardens to get to their yard and to the slate-covered tower where they raised hunting birds.

The Decazes family was so rich that their wealth pushed the limits of decency. Hypocrisy was the distinguished fruit of their large income, but if they acted indifferent about it, it was less from natural pride than it was from a banker's snobbism. I made it a point to ignore them. Gerard, on the other hand, had hated them since his father had humiliated him in front of the Decazes' youngest sons. They were two boys our age, handsome enough, but full of themselves. They spent their vacations going from one party to the next with the rest of the town's "in crowd." They took Gerard for a ruffian, but seemed to envy him a bit, to judge from the pleasure that they took when seeing him shamed by his dad. My cousin would not forgive his father for upholding them as an example, nor would he pardon the boys for being the incarnation of fatherly ideals. Their twenty-year-old brother and younger sister were, on the other hand, our friends. The boy, whose name was Michel, seemed wholesome. Our parents thought he and the whole Decazes clan to be the cat's meow. All of our parents socialized together so often that Gerard facetiously suggested that we display the Decazes' family crest in our home, because, he said, it was more likely that Vespasian spoke only of perfume than that they didn't have a coat of arms. Whenever they visited, we made sure to, as the expression goes, fly the coop, which Gerard acted out by flapping his arms each time we escaped.

We approached the dovecote. The profile of the bluish-colored tower was visible between two trees. It was next to a long greenhouse, and had skylights on the roof. Gerard took out a short German-made dagger that we had found in an army-navy store and whose sheath he had slipped into his belt. He picked up stones, opened the little door to the building, and in the darkness whispered to me, "Come on."

It was starting to get really dark. I entered. The skylight let the pale light of dusk filter into the large room where there were feeding troughs on the ground. These were filled with dark water in which bits of bloody meat floated. The little scavengers had gorged themselves, and the shredded cadavers of their feast were strewn about.

There was a stirring of wings on the metal bars. The falcons and hawks were plunged in the silence that is the harbinger of sleep. Eyes flashed; several birds flew to the roof, with a sudden flap of their wings.

The water started to shine, just for an instant, as if all the light were hiding there, having taken fright. I walked on squishy pieces of meat and felt disgusted. I still had the slingshot, so Gerard handed me some pebbles. "Take down those who are at the top first, and don't worry about the noise. No one is nearby."

About fifteen feet away, the birds formed a dark and quiet line. The first three fell without the others even stirring, the stones hitting them right in the throat, with a dull sound that was low and almost like a caress. The fourth stone struck the perch; with a worried rattle, a falcon took off, and then landed near the still warm birds that I had just killed. I shot one last time. Its little head was torn off; blood spurted all over the bird's wings.

I went out to look for more ammunition, leaving Gerard in a storm of squawking. The birds shrieked, going mad; beaks and claws beat against the wire-reinforced windows and swooped down on Gerard from above, as if attacking a prey.

When I got back, cracking open the door so as to stop the birds from getting out, cries of fury and despair filled the birdhouse. Cut wings and palpitating flesh were strewn about on the dirt floor. Tail feathers stuck to the walls and one of them, alone, delicate, floated on the water of the feeder, bobbing about like Tristan's black sail on the sea.

Gerard had his back up against the windowed door that led to the greenhouse, defending himself, raising his arms and flailing his forearms to protect himself from the biting beaks, trying to stop them from reaching his face. Suddenly, he relaxed, piercing a neck or slicing a throat with the blow of his blade, hot blood covering his hands. It was also all over his chest, which was no longer protected by his tattered shirt, and at the bottom of his cheek near the corner of his mouth. Now and again, he licked it off . . .

Unleashed, he grabbed at the bars, overturned the feeder, and walked on the corpses. His socks, shoes, and jeans were soaked with blood. The sparrow hawks flew about, willy-nilly, stalling at the very top against the skylight and then falling upon him, claws first. Gerard pursued them relentlessly, overtaking one after the other, wounding but not killing them, so that he could go after other victims more quickly. Blood reddened his sweat. Feathers stuck in his hair. The hunt continued. Soon he had killed all living things. He stood very straight and still before his carnage as if he had vanquished the Chimera, the dagger still in his fist.

He slit the throats of the last few birds that were still moving, and then, intoxicated, staggered about in the velvety odor of the dead animals. Blood was smeared all over him. His hands and forearms were covered with lacerations.

I broke two of the skylights' panes with my slingshot; the cold night air grabbed hold of the smell of the dead birds and took it away, as if to savor it alone in the shadows.

We stopped in the barn on the way home. Now and again, Gerard would shiver from his head to his toes. I thought he was cold until I touched him. Under his torn shirt and on his back, he was covered with sweat. His heart was beating fast, so I laid him down in the hay. In the shadows I looked for his eyes. His breath guided me. I took the mouth of this wild boy who was enveloped by the smell of his efforts and, despite a night as black as coal, like nights without stars, I recognized his sullen profile and his large melancholy eyes. He was soon naked between my arms. The shadows hid the bloodstains from me, but even if the darkness stole their color from me, the darker brown on certain parts of his skin reminded me of them. I kept quiet, and this Parsifalian body covered with blood and dirt and troubling charm filled me with desire and horror. In the blackness, he understood that his savagery had suddenly revealed to me a cruel Gerard, pitiless like a murderer after his first taste of blood. Now he knew that punishment would come. I remained silent, but I owed it to my loyalty and to my love to punish him. I waited for his revolt against the disdain in which my silence was holding him to make him distance himself from my body, or to make him utter words of repentance. Pride kept him still for a long time. Shadows bathed him in that voluptuous light in which each gesture seemed to blossom. At last, he lowered his head. I took hold of his throat, picked him up, and pushed his head back while gripping his short hair in my left fist. I commanded him, in a flat voice: "On your knees."

He knelt. With one leg I steadied his body and, without him making one move to defend himself, I hit him with the back of my hand. We could hear nothing besides our breathing. He parsed his lips. I hit him with all my might, slapping his head from one side to the other with my furious hand. I hit him without stopping, so hard that I no longer knew who I was, where I was, or what was happening. My palm stung and I thought it was filled with blood. I stopped.

A sob told me that it was not with blood, but with tears that Gerard's face was covered. I bent his head back once more and began to hit him again. One of his hands pressed against my thigh to ask for mercy, but it was only my dwindling force that stopped this game. I let go of him, looking for words to hurt him instead. "You are a cruel son of a bitch. You have no heart. To see you give into your animal instincts so quickly makes me wonder what you wouldn't do."

Gerard sprung up, rebelling all of a sudden, his voice trembling: "You are going to ask for my forgiveness immediately, or I'll destroy you and with you, the love you feel for me!"

After a moment, I murmured, "I'm sorry . . ."

Outside the wind blew through the yard like a young lover who has died of worry. We slipped noiselessly into the house. Gerard was now shivering because of the cold. In the light of the bedroom, you could see the marks of my hand on his face, his shirt in ribbons, his legs and shoulders stained with blood. He undressed. The dirty halo of sweat and blood had dried on his body with a vulgar seductiveness. He lay facedown on the bed, his head in his hands, and forgot about me. I turned off the light. Through the window that we had left partially open even though Gerard was freezing came the sound of the wind, raging, filled with dust and the smell of trees and the earth. All of nature was trembling. At certain moments, you could hear the forest shudder from deep within. The pond would be dark and covered with foam.

A bolt of lightning flashed at the horizon, followed by others, whiter and briefer. A gust of wind stamped out a rain shower. The moon appeared, only to disappear again. Suddenly, sheets of rain surged from the sky; the wind blew the windows open. The gravel around the house crackled. On the veranda, the water played a melancholy march of an abandoned lover. The trees rustled and creaked. The lightning, redoubling its splendor, violently illuminated the bedroom, in one second showing me the whole valley, the faraway hills, the nearby trees, a clearer and more perfect image than would have been seen in the middle of the day. And, as if its target had been this prostrate boy, it threw itself upon his defenseless body. The light streamed over his legs and the backs of his knees, inundating his back and drawing the stark shadow of his buttocks on his kidneys.

I lay down next to him. The storm put on an incredible show all night, forcing us to keep our eyes open.

It turned out to be a fortuitous storm, to which my uncle attributed his disasters. In the days that followed, the Decazes boys didn't say a peep about their birds of prey. The storm must have helped them get rid of the remains and allowed them to explain the killing and the escape of the remaining birds to their parents. But they weren't dupes, and already they were paying more attention to Gerard than usual, which meant that he definitely figured in their nefarious plans.

While waiting to see what would happen, Gerard and I were content to love each other.

IV

I often woke suddenly at dawn, and before falling back to sleep, I evoked for myself all that belonged to my past. It was as if a new existence made me be reborn with the dawn; I saw everything underneath my closed eyelids, as clearly as if nothing else could have happened. Solitude had shaped my heart; between Gerard and me the pride of love had degenerated into haughtiness. We separated from each other right at the point when our proximity would have meant more than just the neighborly heat of our bodies . . .

We arrived at Amboise on Thursday evening; by the next day we were settled in for the whole summer. An empty room where fruit and herbs for tea were dried separated Gerard's room from mine. We were alone on that floor. The garden was vast; the summer weighed it down with the hours that seemed to hide themselves in the increasingly dark shadows. The heat crushed the garden, while lightening it at the same time by making the expanses of grass undulate from the ground up as if the air was carrying them away in its sparkling river.

I couldn't give Gerard up, and left him only for the pleasure of finding him again. We were together from the moment we got out of bed: one can't wait when one is in love. No matter how numerous were our longing looks, no matter how much time we spent together, there were times when we were apart because of sleep or because of the detours that life imposes on those who wait for each other.

We had peaches and fruit juice for breakfast, while still in our pajamas. Afterward, we took turns in the bathroom without bothering to shut the door. Each person respected the nakedness of the other by speaking to him without seeing him, not because of prudishness, but because of desire. Only once did I enter the bathroom, because Gerard had cried out. He had hurt himself falling against the soap dish. He was bent over, his hands on his thigh, his back covered with water drops, and his round buttocks glowing with water. I helped him out of the tub. There were a few drops of blood; he had scraped himself slightly while standing up. It hurt, so I painted the wound with Mercurochrome. It looked as if two painted lips had been placed there.

In this way, the first week was a game of hide-and-seek. Things I said to him subsequently deformed themselves in my head. In my imagination, I created conversations filled with words of passion that I wasn't entirely sure not to have said, but that I would have been happy to keep to myself. I was uneasy: wanting to, but not wanting to; in love, but feeling hostile; always desperate until the point where some impulse would drive me to him, resolved to convince him, to violate his heart. Then he would look at me, and I would change the subject. We were hiding in broad daylight. I loved him with the insanity that characterizes a first love. His sudden blush when I contemplated him looked like vanity to me. I should have recognized that it was an unrealized confession.

It was enough simply to exist next to him. All the while laying down my arms before the person to whom I was submitting myself, I had conquered him. Everything—the summer, our free time—was reduced to one utterance, which for lovers is the gateway to the world: "I love you." This "Open, sesame!" was the password to all our treasures. Even so, we hesitated to claim these riches that could be ours with these simple magic words. Love trampled on pride and on everything that wasn't love itself. In a week, it turned us into men.

After his bath, Gerard went to work in his room. I read, but not the book that was opened in front of me; I was reading instead the one that I was writing in my heart. We chatted every five minutes or so. Gerard approached his studies with a kangaroo-like energy: with a bound, he was far from his books; two leaps more and he was deeply involved in them. At two o' clock, on days when it was too hot, we would take naps on the grass. When the ardor of the afternoon diminished around five, we played tennis or, unmooring a leaky skiff, drifted about on the Loire between the yellow sky and the golden water.

Gerard dozed in the boat. When, tired of rowing, I reproached him for his indolence, he stood up, his wet bathing suit stuck to his bottom, and amused himself by fooling about with the oars. The landscape looked liquid between his legs. The color of his flesh threw it into a blue-gray fog. Once, I put my forehead against his knees. Gerard let go of the oars, grabbed hold of my neck, and pulled my head along the inside of his thighs. I resisted. His crotch smelled warm and musky, like that of a young buck. He traced his body with my mouth, from his curving stomach to his chest. Then he pushed me backward, making me lose my balance and topple into the water. Our game couldn't go any further.

I swam to the bank, where I had to take off my shirt and shorts. I crossed the outskirts in my underwear. Gerard, who had joined me, found this funny. "You're indecent. You're walking around without waiting to dry to get peoples' attention! Whose eye are you hoping to catch?" When we arrived in our yard, he said, "I'm going to go get some stuff for you to change into. If either your dad or mine sees you, God knows what they'll think! Go into the barn. But, there's a catch: give me your underwear. I'll put everything out to dry."

"You jerk! I'll get my revenge." I gave in, threw my underwear on the ground before him who had the indecency to say, for the first time, "Hey, you've got a nice body. I'll come back with what you need in order to hide this eighth wonder of the world from me." He disappeared with a laugh, which afterward, upon reflection, seemed like a troubled laugh to me.

While waiting for him, I thought about throwing myself at his knees, giving myself up to him, confessing everything. When he came back, however, I got dressed, pretending to have forgotten everything.

A week later we still hadn't made much progress on our path toward happiness. The week after that, I wasn't hungry. For no reason I started shivering after having been burning up only shortly before, as if I had gotten too much sun. Our fathers, who were still satisfied by our lies, saw nothing, because I was able to control myself. My body was nothing but sighs. I fought against my tears when I found myself alone. I couldn't do without Gerard, from whom I fled for no reason. He was acting the same way. He seemed moody to me. I realized that he wasn't eating at all, that his face was looking rather hollowed out, that his eyes were bigger and were half-encircled by dark rings on his cheekbones. He didn't come into my room anymore unless he was clothed. Without any kind of formal arrangement, we began to use the bathroom at different times. We both pretended that nothing had changed.

Saturday the heat was particularly cruel. The air was filled with insects. People kept their houses closed in order to keep the coolness inside. Our contrary spirits incited Gerard and me to go out, despite it all. We decided to go for a swim in the river. A gentle vapor made the banks seem as if they were trembling.

The water was warm. I dove in right away. When I resurfaced, Gerard was floating about, his hair wet only at his temples. I approached and grabbed him, so he'd sink. He struggled and was forced under. I followed the outline of his body in the green water. I kept heading toward him, able to make out only the top of his chest since the cloudy water obscured the rest of him. I tried to grab his body in my arms. He struggled like a demon, but laughed as he ran away. I was able to grab him around the waist. Without realizing it, I had a hold of the tie to his bathing suit. I pulled it, and Gerard swam away leaving me with his trunks.

I went back to the place where we'd left our stuff and dried myself off calmly. Gerard dove again and again, trying to find his bathing suit. He gave up and gamely walked straight toward me. Water was running with regret from his torso. When there was none left except on his ankles, he stood still before my eyes, against the green background of the trees, his arms barely folded. His hair curled in the air's caress, the water having finished its loving touch. The flesh of his thighs glowed because of the bath, and gleamed there where the sun touched it through the leaves. A vein crossed his leg under his knee. Another swelled down his forearm toward his wrist. For some inexplicable reason, I didn't seize the opportunity to avenge myself, even though destiny had offered nudity's alibi to our senses twice already...

He chose that night to try to overcome the obstacle. After a rather humid day, the night was going to be absolutely suffocating. I rested on my bed, unable to fall asleep. The moon, already high and clear in the sky, illuminated everything with a pale but strong light, which seemed to emanate from things and make them leap from their shadows. In my room, since the moonlight didn't come in directly but rather at an angle, only the panes of the windows were glowing.

    Gerard entered after midnight and asked if I was asleep. I told him I wasn't. He came near my bed and sat down. The red bottoms of his pajamas looked black against the whiteness of the sheet on which I lay. We said hardly a word to each other.

    I was afraid of being betrayed by my penis. In order to stop my cousin from seeing it, I ended up turning over onto my stomach and pretended to go to sleep. So, he got up without a sound. Before leaving the room, however, since the moonlight fell at my feet and lit up one leg, he touched it and then stopped when he got to my shoulder. I kept pretending to sleep through my lie. When I was alone, my body was so upset that I rubbed my chest against the sheets, and then drew myself up against the white light in order to call forth another whiteness . . .

    Sunday morning was quiet. Large clouds brought shade and a western breeze. I went to church on Sundays to listen to the music, without thinking about anything else. Gerard didn't believe in anything and stayed in bed.

    Like the first two Sundays of our vacation, I went to Amboise. Gerard wasn't up. My father took my cousin and me in the car. I hadn't told Gerard where I was going. I don't know why, but I felt a sinking sense of presentiment in my chest during the service. I left my father at the end of the mass. He went to the bakery with my cousin, and then ran some other errands until noontime. When I returned, the house was empty. My uncle was watering the plants. Gerard was nowhere to be found. I went to the riverbank: no trace of him. I went to our room. The orderliness of it was unusual. I thought of the barn: no one there, either. As soon as I entered our yard, however, an interior voice told me to go back, so I returned to the barn. In a recess filled with rusty tools on the other side of the hay bales, Gerard lay facedown.

    I called him. I knelt down next to him and turned him over. His body didn't show any wounds, but his heart had almost stopped beating. I could smell something coming from his half-open mouth; an earthy green odor turned my stomach. There wasn't a moment to lose. I took off my shirt, put his head against my chest, and stuck my fingers far down his throat. There was a contraction and suddenly a jet of blackish liquid covered my arms. Gerard opened his eyes. He couldn't stop vomiting. I thought I would faint. Rivulets of bile ran down my thigh. He was covered in sweat. I dried him off, took off his shirt, and gave him mine. He sat there dazed, his back against a low beam.

I retched myself and then headed toward the door. Gerard saw me, and tried to get up. "I'm okay," he said. "Go ahead. I know you're disgusted." I rebelled and, in order to prove to him that nothing could repulse me, kissed him on his humid lips and led him toward his room. Once he was in bed, I went back to the barn and looked around: there were crushed yellow petals on the ground where he had fallen. He had picked an ordinary tobacco flower, and swallowed it pistil and all, believing that he could kill himself this way. The idea of his death was a kind of death. Why? Because he couldn't live as he wanted to, he told me, refusing to explain any further. It was proof of his love, because a lover hates time, since it is always stealing the one he loves from him.

Gerard stayed in bed the entire afternoon. I covered for him as best as I could, saying that he had a toothache, which was met with the ironic response, "If only it were a wisdom tooth!" By evening he was doing better. His misadventure was visible in his face only in the deeper radiance in his eyes and a palpable melancholy that I attributed to the passage of death between us. One can often see a strange presence in a lover's face that makes it seem as if the face of the one he loves has been placed like a mask on his features, so much does his flesh long for that of the other. Gerard lived with my lips on his own; sometimes I couldn't recognize him anymore.

This failed suicide was a sign. The hurricane was approaching. Like sailors when they see the proverbial red sky at night not knowing if the next morning's dawn will bring a day of calm or a storm, we waited unawares for love's torments. It would take yet another summer day for this story of untroubled lovers to begin with one adolescent slumbering and the other maintaining a troubled teenage vigil.

This is what I thought about when I opened my eyes at dawn, and during the first two weeks of vacation, which had shown me unexpected pleasures. I got up at eight o'clock, my head filled with the noises of passion that makes memories as sonorous as kisses. The massacre of the hawks seemed a long time ago. I was supposed to go to Amboise that afternoon to buy some records. Gerard had promised to wait for me in the barn, which was our hideout, and to stay busy reading some crime story or other. When I arrived in the bathroom, he was naked. Soapsuds covered the back of his neck like lace. The sun entered in waves through the open window, making the bubbles scintillate. Gerard smelled like clean skin, his smile was as bright as could be, and his eyes were tender. It was as if the morning ablution had destroyed the voluptuous shadows of the night and had offered this child god to the new day. He had scrubbed himself so hard that he was pink.

When I eventually got out of the water myself, Gerard was combing his hair in front of the mirror with no clothes on. His muscles were swollen by the push-ups he'd been doing. Love must have offered me this beautiful boy who seemed to come directly from my wildest dreams. In becoming real, he had managed to keep some kind of mysterious glow.

"I want to give you some of my blood," he said. He took a hunting knife from the pile of clothes that we had carelessly left on the chair. We exchanged blood through two shallow gashes.

I drank this red force that came impetuously to my mouth in spurts. The future opened like an immense door before us, through which we entered the palace of love, like children in a forest.

Once we were dressed, we stretched out on the bed. For the first time, Gerard trusted me and talked to me about the future.

"What are you planning on doing? Me, I'm going to try to pass the bac again, and we'll stay together. After that, I don't think I could deal with being separated. You're seventeen; you've got to know what you want."

The question about "what I was planning to do" kept coming up. It was as if I was banging my head against a wall because Gerard just wouldn't let up. I thought I could finally answer him sensibly, despite the impulse of my heart: "Listen, we have to live for the present. We're on vacation. Let's love each other on vacation. Once the summer is over, we'll see. You are the summer. I love you, and that should be enough for you. The rest is nothing."

This isn't what he wanted to hear. He was waiting for something more definitive. "I want to know what you think, what you know, what you are feeling, and what you want. I want to be you. When I'm in your arms, I couldn't give a damn about the rest. I don't know anything but love. I adore you. It's your life that I want, all of it. And I don't want you to have anything but mine." Suddenly, he said, "Let's make a pledge to each other." And then, "No, that's too stupid. I already swear my allegiance to you."

I was stupefied with happiness. The mysterious Gerard gave me his heart with the same ardor with which he gave me his body. I discovered that he wanted me to take everything from him. I was sincere when I tried to attenuate his enthusiasm by throwing the ashes of the uncertain future on his fire. Gerard was fickle; I wanted to test him. I spoke to him quietly: "I adore you, too. I'm only thinking about the here and now. Let's not look any further ahead. . . . Your heart could change. I don't know anything about the people you've loved before me. You, you're my first love. And besides, it's possible that you'll like girls when you're twenty. Maybe I'll be dead then, or we'll live far from each other. Even if you haven't changed, even if I'm still in love with you, we'll see things so differently that it won't seem possible anymore to tackle it together. Love me as I love you: our happiness is now." I spoke to him so quietly that I could barely hear myself. Gerard pressed himself against me. "I'll always love you," he murmured, "even dead."

I looked at him. Tears were streaming down his cheeks.

One night, when he was dreaming, I put my ear against his chest where his heart was. He said some unintelligible words, which practically leapt out of him. It was as if he was falling with them into an abyss from the top of the mountain that is sleep. I tried to surprise the other Gerard, the one I would never know unless I were able finally to overcome that thin barrier of skin at last and to become the flesh itself. I wanted a perfect twin, which love sometimes gave me in the middle of the night . . .

V

The town of Amboise led a double life during the summer, its identity varying with the hours. The sunny morning hours were rumor-filled. These gave way to the dull hours of the arid afternoon when the shadows spread themselves out lazily on the crackled ground. Later the softness of the dusk allowed people to go out again. For a few fleeting evenings the troubled atmosphere of nocturnal places invaded a city that had been agitated by the summer, as if it needed the calm of the early evening to satisfy the curiosities of its heart.

I knew only the morning hours, when you could already make out the impending beauty of the day from the calm blue sky, and from the indeterminate place from which the light came. You couldn't quite make out the disk that was the sun, which moved its fiery mass and made the air around it tremble. I discovered that the afternoon was silent and mostly colorless because the gloomy dejection of the heat enveloped the houses and trees with a shroud of gray-gold. Sweat ran down my chest and made it glisten. The shop windows reflected a seductive vision of myself, but as if from the depths of a watery mirror. I encountered only playing children wearing immense straw hats, and old women dressed in the somber twill that you don't see anymore except in the country. These shadows brought me back, thanks to I don't know what secret mechanism of thought, to my cousin whom I had left reading. God, I was crazy about him, as I was crazy about the brutal caresses that he gave me because he thought that they could hide his tenderness. Gerard was love. Gerard was my love. I didn't want to know anything about his past, about the small savage beast that he kept deep down inside who had been fondled by plenty of other boys. His haughty adolescent air made me sense that he was used to compliments. He charmed people with a flightiness that made it all too easy to imagine the voluptuous concessions that he had made. When you were in his arms, however, he plied you into the shape dictated by his desires.

I wandered leisurely in the streets, isolated by my love, not seeing the half-closed shutters through which one side of the town spied on the other. Both halves were unaware of my hidden life, because for me, life was summed up in just one face. I wasn't in Amboise; I was at the foot of Gerard's bed. I looked at him. He looked at me over his bent knees, his legs spread. I saw him everywhere around me.

Eventually I pushed open the door to the record shop. It was run by a nice young guy, handsome enough, whose store seemed more like a cave because the blue and green shades that protected the store window gave the light that entered the shop a weird, unexpected luminosity reminiscent of certain underwater caves whose only light came from the azure reverberations of the day on the sea. Whirlpools, or more accurately, cascades of music that the listening cabins couldn't quite contain increased the illusion, which was completed by the owner, whose sun-darkened face made one think of those vigorous sailors so sought after by the emperors of decadent Rome for their personal caprices. He found Gerard attractive. My cousin had come to the store with me one morning, and without caring a bit about the album that I wanted to listen to, he started to talk to the guy with the express purpose of seducing him. Afterward I skewered him for this girlish behavior with such perfect accuracy that he didn't go to town with me after that. The record seller must have suffered, because he had seen Gerard, had listened to him, and since then had always figured out a way to bring the conversation around to my cousin.

He showed me several new recordings that I refused disinterestedly. I listened to the beginning of a John Cage album, bought it, and left the shop. I felt suddenly tired, and since I'd been walking in the strong sun for a little while already, felt the need to rest in the shade a bit. I was not far from a church. A miniscule black hearse stood in a dark corner like those old ploughs that sit rusting in the fields all summer. Under the portals, crowns of red gladiolas wilted. As soon as I entered the building, the coolness struck me.

I stood upright against a pillar of the church, which was dark because of the fake Italianate arches that opened their black squares up onto the knave. The stained-glass windows, which should have been aflame on such a bright day, threw only a feeble blue light because the neighboring houses' proximity blocked the light. Candles illuminated the chorus. Their flames cut fugitive petals in the wax. It was so dark that I couldn't see anything beyond a black catafalque that stood among six funereal candelabras. Now and again, you could hear the organ accompany the prayers. There was a moment of silence, and then a disembodied contralto voice threw the first words of the Dies Irae into the knave.

"Day of wrath, this day will make the earth a land of ashes, as with David and the Sibyll . . ." In the twilight I listened to the silent dialogue that was taking place inside me as my heart responded.

I envisioned a wrinkled old woman, who was nevertheless darkly majestic. The black folds of her billowing, unbelted dress enveloped her. This vision mingled with one of a king in a large crown. He held a book in his left hand in which Gerard's face was drawn right next to my own.

"Yes," said the voices to one another, "yes, day of wrath, this day when your passion will be no more than those of two corpses."

"What horror will be yours, when you are condemned for believing in your bond . . ."

This implacable voice destroyed any words of love that I might have uttered. The faith inherent in this love was so profound, however, that I understood it to be eternal, lasting even after Gerard's death. Gerard didn't share this feeling. I guess I didn't really, either, since what I felt was not as I had been taught to believe. I didn't respect people for whom faith seemed to be just a habit, nor did I respect those who were ready to throw themselves into any old church simply because they were afraid of themselves. My faith existed only in the most obscure depths of my heart. Just like a diamond, the hard ground and raw carbon of ten-million-year-old petrified forest weren't enough to form my beliefs. The whole force of nature was necessary: its noises, its ferns, its birds, all of which are brutally cast into the bowels of the earth, and which are lit by countless centuries' worth of stars. This is what makes a brilliant, reflective surface of belief. This is why my faith needed an inevitable, inescapable love to solidify it.

As for Gerard, his religion was love. Sometimes he seemed to be aware of a life of which ours seemed but a mere shadow. For him, believing was loving. Pressing himself against a body like his own transfigured him to the point that when I held him, I felt as though I had a god in my arms. The youthful beauty of his body allowed one to get nearer to that secret Gerard, to what one would call his soul. His curly hair, his little ears, the nape of his neck: these weren't only the external signs of desire. They were also the instruments of a sacred love that used beauty in order to enslave the heart forever. Our kisses weren't merely physical caresses. I wanted to make love to the invisible Gerard. And yet, the deceitful softness of the flesh distanced me from it each time.

"Unhappy is he whose face will be clouded and dark. He will be judged by himself, and will be inexorable . . ." I was listening to my own funeral mass. These candles, the organ, the flowers, they were all for me. It was my death. The Dies Irae finished with supplications and vehement harmonies from the organ, while another voice surged within me. "Day of wrath, this day of your death. You will be judged by love, and love will neither spare nor pity you or those hours that were yours. It will not justify forgetting, except during moments of rest. What it wants is to know, to be intimately acquainted with those thoughts that furrow your brow, those unspoken desires, the cries of a love guarded in the breast, in those solitary gestures, those glimmers of rejoicing, the dimensions of hope. The air that you breathe would make other men's hearts burst. With Gerard, that which is suffocating becomes as light as air. His blood demands an inferno! He is love, and will not condemn you."

All of a sudden, I had a presentiment of a future unhappiness. I had to go home; Gerard was calling me. I turned over a chair on my way, and the noise was audible throughout the church. Once outside, the sun's rays whipped me. As soon as I was on the road again, however, the silence of the day instantly chased away these black feelings. I decided not to go directly home. The smells of summer made me linger on the way. There were wildflowers in the humid ditch. The air was saturated with the intoxicating smell of fresh-cut wheat.

In the barn, in the middle of the hay, lay Gerard's book, still open. His room was empty, so I went to mine. I knew he was there as soon as I opened the door because the curtains were closed.

"Is that you, Pierre?" he said.

He was lying facedown on the bed, still naked. He begged me not to let the light in. I approached him, and took his face in my hands. His lips were swollen, and from his nose there was a trace of blood that ran to his lips.

"They grabbed me and beat me," he said, his voice trembling with anger. That was all he would tell me.

At dinner, he wore long sleeves, and no one noticed anything. Politics was the topic of conversation, and we made fun of them, as usual. At ten he went to bed. The branches of the trees were still bathed in the twilight. He tossed and turned endlessly, murmuring contextless words, whose meaning I grasped only now and again. I heard, "No, I don't want to." Slowly, I was able to piece together what had happened from these shards of sentences grasped from a bad dream. He was terribly restless, his face bathed in sweat. He couldn't bear to stay on his back, which was covered with red scratches and welts, as were his arms and legs. His raw and broken flesh had caused him to throw off the covers. He must have been suffering at the dinner table, because out of a sense of pride, he had worn a scratchy pair of linen trousers that must have burned against his buttocks and thighs and a shirt that was too light to hide the stripes of the riding crop on his shoulder.

This is what I imagined: At the start of the afternoon, Gerard was holed up in the barn, reading his detective story as usual. He heard someone call, and thinking it was I called back, "Here I am." Philippe, one of the Decazes brothers, came in, leaving the door open behind him so his brothers could follow. They'd planned their attack with care. The other brothers waited outside, along with the two boys with whom we'd played tennis.

"Where is Pierre?" he asked.

Gerard made a vague gesture without looking up from his book. Philippe, coming closer, fell on him with all his weight. My cousin fought back, but the others joined in, grabbing his wrists and his ankles, covering his mouth with some adhesive tape, and took their victim toward the dovecote.

The door to the tower was closed and double-bolted. They undid the ropes around his feet so Gerard could stand up. They ripped off the tape, and one of them stood behind him to prepare him for torture: he unbuttoned his shirt and pulled it down to his wrists. Then he attacked his blue jeans, touching Gerard's penis by mistake and making him shiver. As soon as they'd pulled down his zipper and his underpants, my cousin hit him with his bound hands right in the face. A melee ensued: Gerard, immobilized, spit in their faces. The boys became furious and beat him with his own belt, and then, as much because he was beautiful as because he was rebellious, they hit him hard enough to draw blood on his thighs, his back, his arms, and his ass.

Gerard became dizzy. Did he have any idea of the secret meeting that had been planned expressly for the purpose of using him for their pleasure? Excited by their blows, the boys imagined using him like a girl, one after the other. Cast to the ground, Gerard stopped moving. A blow to the neck with the belt had stunned him. The boys quickly took off their jeans. Their heavy, dark thighs emerged from their pants, and the air around them became hotter. In order to cum more easily, they took off their short-sleeved shirts that were covering their asses. Gerard was at their feet, facedown. They contemplated him for a moment. Then the first one put his mouth against the nape of his neck . . .

I didn't want to know anything more. Worried by the palpitations of my heart, I murmured: "You are turning me on. The night is long when you're asleep, but you are mine more than you are during the day. Love is violence. I'm jealous of what those guys did to you."

Gerard slept like the dead. His shadowy hand lay open, ready to be kissed. Touched by pleasure, he was no longer Gerard. Pleasure's flesh had substituted itself for his own, making him no longer a boy of flesh and blood, but the incarnation of masculine pleasure. It was as if there were some strange agreement between his flesh and pleasure that created this creature for whom the name Gerard no longer fit—at least not the name *Gerard* that I had so often tenderly pronounced. I was driven mad by the fact that hands other than my own had touched him. The person those boys had abused was me. Gerard's gestures penetrated my own to such a degree that I was no longer able to recognize myself. With that servile imitation so common to lovers, I bitterly admired his rage. In vain I would have pulled him from the night. His touch didn't satisfy me anymore. I needed an infinite gesture that neither time nor shadow would destroy. Each second threw my derisory caresses back in my face. I had to start again so as not to stop being aware of the body lying next to me, embraced in the invisible arms of some dream. Sleep was the lover who stole Gerard from me. Gerard tossed and turned, groaning occasionally until morning.

It was already light out when the noises of the country gave way to the cock crows that woke us. The water burned his skin so that Gerard couldn't wash himself, so I powdered his back with talcum. Today as well he had to give in and wear a suit for the meal, but as soon as he returned to his room, he ripped off his torturous clothing.

I left him for a little while in the afternoon in order to poke around the attic. He joined me there, voluble: "Listen," he said, "you won't believe what I just heard as I went by the living room. I couldn't help myself and put my ear to the keyhole. Your father and mine were both there. So was Madame Palin, Madame Decazes, and two or three other important people"—at this point, he aped a worldly tone—"from the environs. They were talking about some stuff, and here's what I heard . . ."

Then, quickly varying his poses, with a virtuosity and a gravity of which I hadn't thought him capable, he brought to life in that suitcase-filled attic, a distinguished "salon" replete with all its idiocy, its ennui, and its self-satisfaction. He indicated which part he was playing by modulating his voice.

"*Your father* (serious and with his hand in his jacket pocket): 'I am very careful to make sure that such publications do not fall into the hands of my son. This type of reading could provoke him to run after God knows what sort of girl. This is hardly what we have in mind for him.'

"*Madame Palin* (a tone higher, with a clipped pronunciation, as in lower Brittany): 'I find the entire thing so disturbing that it's difficult for me even to believe what people are saying.'

"*My father* (who up until now had been digging some playing cards out of a vase into which I'd thrown them the day before yesterday): 'And what exactly are they saying?'

"*Madame Palin:* 'One really can't take any heed of such nonsense. It is, however, what the children of our friends have told us. Isn't that so, Geraldine?'

"*Madame Decazes* (in a saccharine voice): 'The whole thing is completely silly. Let's forget it.'

"*Your father* (curious all the same): 'Oh! It's just between us. You needn't worry. We would, however, appreciate a little light on the situation.'

"*Madame Decazes* (somewhat excitedly): 'Well! I'm only telling you this because I cannot believe it. What kind of influence do you think that your son's cousin is having on him? Isn't Gerard, well, a bit perverted? A little funny?'

"*My father* (rather furious to see me described this way): 'What a strange choice of words!'

"*Madame Palin* (amiably helping her troubled friend with her own admission): 'Their games are making them rather scornful of the company of their peers. Neither my sons nor Geraldine's have managed to tame them. I can't help thinking that Gerard's the one to blame. They're content with each other, so it seems. I can't imagine it could be anything else, given the way they stare into each other's eyes for hours, even when they're around other people.'

"*Your father* (not wanting to understand): 'They're just plotting something. You're making a mountain out of a molehill.'

"*Madame Decazes:* 'What about their midnight strolls?'

"*Madame Ricard* (who hadn't missed a word, even though she'd been busy flirting with the doctor): 'Running away from others at that age is typical of what Freud would call "exclusive affections."'

"*My father:* 'Gerard is studying with Pierre for the exam he's going to take in October. He failed when he took it this July, and Pierre nicely offered to spend the summer here, so that he could help his cousin.'

"*Madame Decazes:* 'I didn't know that you could study for the bac by kissing your cousin on the mouth one hundred yards in front of the house.'

"I stopped listening, 'cause it was just too stupid." I could tell that Gerard was lying because he'd turned white as a ghost.

The shadow of death entered the attic in this way. On the outside, it was just a cloud that passed in front of the eyebrow window. This sudden darkness that came after the golden rays in which the dust had been dancing was hiding a person who was following our every move. I could hear his furtive footsteps echo in my heart; day after day they became louder, more self-assured, and then it would be the end. My heart would burst because there was too much of an uproar in it. I put my hand on Gerard's chest. It was as if something inside was knocking to get out of him and inside me.

Our fathers didn't say a word. For our part, we just gave into our carnal love, but it was a love over which birds of prey endlessly circled.

VI

"Pierre, Pierre!" My name had become a scream. I had decided to hide myself in order to watch while I was supposed to be waiting for Gerard. He looked around him confusedly, worried because I was supposed to be there. A thrush's call broke the silence. Gerard called me again, and then said my name just once so quietly that I could tell he had said it only by the movement of his lips. Then he took off, stumbling over the tree roots that lined the path. He sat against a tree, or rather, he let himself slide down the trunk and let his head fall against it. Among the leaves, from inside the thicket in which I hid, I could see his mouth and neck, two places where I would have liked to put my lips. What was he thinking about?

I wanted to run to him, to tell him it was just a joke, but the cruelty that is the basis of all real love held me back. I wanted to spy on him, to see what he was like when he thought he was alone. I wanted to know if I was going to see someone whom I wouldn't love. There were moments when I wanted to empty my heart, to erase the image of love imprinted on it. I wanted to wipe out the face that I saw from within even when my eyes were closed.

He took off toward the house, head lowered, kicking rocks dejectedly. His body was imbued with an indefinable sadness. At last he disappeared behind the barn, at which point the sun went out for me. The trees stopped moving. I didn't feel a thing. I looked without sensing anything. I listened without living, my throat constricted. Gerard's solitude took possession of my body. The ardent day that had overwhelmed me with beauty became suddenly dismal. The green shivering spring, the cool and dark woods were still there before me, but now cursed; Gerard had taken their soul with them when he left. The farther he got from me, the more acutely I became aware of the distress of this boy who was looking to make his first confessions.

I had had enough. In our most nocturnal fiery embraces I had imagined saying words that never crossed my lips. The vulgar words of love were easier. They only engaged the body. My loneliness now resembled Gerard. I ran to him; my desire arrived before I did. On the way, I tried to remember what his face looked like. Sometimes I couldn't. Other times, I could see him before me, but only with some fleeting expression or momentary attitude. His mirage surrounded me.... A few seconds later, I opened the door to the barn and threw myself on him.

We had a game with crazy rules whose only goal was to enslave the other and to do what you wanted to him physically. The game allowed anything to happen. The garden became a territory where you had to capture the adversary (because we were enemies) through cunning. This time, I acted as if I was just having fun. Before he could defend himself, I'd tied him by the wrists, which I'd then roped to a rusty old nail usually used for hanging saddles. All of a sudden, I hit him. I had taken off my belt with the intention of murdering his ass. What troubled jealousy I displayed in this taste for hurting him exactly where I admired him the most! I didn't undress him, because my blows hurt all the more through his clothes. I would have been afraid that I would give in to my basest hungers too quickly, had he been naked.

"Bastard," he repeated under his breath, "you bastard . . ." His accent was the same as when, in the middle of the night, he would go crazy while underneath me. His voice was as hot as his skin.

I hit him again and again. First came the long whistle of admiration from the belt, then the flat sound of the blow with which the sound of my erratic breathing mixed. Gerard stopped breathing, groaning in pain even before contact with the belt. He only gasped afterward, if the poorly aimed blow had hit bare skin, because I ended up ripping off his shirt in order to see his back and pulling down his jeans around his ankles. I liked him shackled like this, completely in my possession. A vein swelled on the back of his knee, but disappeared each time he gave into this painful pleasure. I found nothing sweeter than caressing him there, putting my lips on the spot for the briefest moment. Slowly he was tamed, and I was able to quicken the pace of my blows without pushing him beyond the limits of his endurance. It was in fact I who was the first to admit defeat because of a terrible ache in my shoulder, and the fear that Gerard would think of me only as an immense, human-faced fist. I finally untied his bruised wrists, after being sure that he had calmed down. The idea of avenging himself could make him incredibly mean.

He smiled. "You hit hard today. What did you eat for breakfast?" Then he carefully fixed me in the gaze of his changing eyes. "If ever you happen to fall into my grasp, you'd better watch out . . . but I wouldn't wait quite so long before I . . ." He didn't finish the sentence, but instead simply buttoned his shirt. Already he had become yet another body among those that peopled my waking hours.

After dinner, my father told me he wanted to have a word with me. Gerard left the room in a bit of a huff. My father sat down and told me to do the same, but I preferred to remain standing. He asked me to return to Paris to register for school on Gerard's behalf while he finished preparing for his exams. As a bribe, he offered me tickets to an English musical group that usually never came to France. I used all of my powers of persuasion: the beauty of our surroundings, our swims, how tiring it would be in the hot city in the middle of the summer. He rebutted that I could have fun by myself in Paris; I countered that it would be suffocating, and told him that the group wasn't supposed to be very good anyway. Besides, it would be so counterproductive to disturb the tranquil routine that we'd established during our working vacation. "Well, you shouldn't let that stop you," said my father. "You should spend the rest of your break in Corsica. You've earned it."

This friendly concern was just cover for a well-thought-out plan to separate me from Gerard. The easily spotted tricks of my father only served to strengthen my resolve not to leave. I couldn't give my own game away, however, and so pretended not to understand what he was up to. He didn't suspect a thing. I left him to find Gerard, who was in his room, dying with worry. All of this was motivated by our fathers' uncertainty about what was really drawing us to each other, despite their efforts, despite life's efforts. Thanks to the fact that it was they themselves who had provided us with a common roof under which to live our passion, it was as if their role in our love story was to be that of our deaf and blind confidants.

I wasn't about to abandon my cousin to the torpid provincial summer, cursed as they are with their houses shut up to keep out the heat, their dark closed churches, their tomblike stillness. Staying with Gerard in this dead land would be a pleasure. We didn't need anything except each other. Like all pleasures, I felt it so intensely that it disappeared with corresponding alacrity. I didn't know how to admit my happiness to him, now that we were in fact sharing it. Desire had already rewarded me. It was often like that with the most common gestures: touching Gerard's body distanced the image of his body being caressed by me. Sliding my tongue between his lips seemed insane, but then it made everything resume its primitive force. Gerard's lips found their softness. Between my hands, his head assumed the brutal air that it had when he came. I discovered a new person each time, and each time my body lost itself in this unknown person. I was afraid of losing him.

When he asked me what had brought my father to this decision, I didn't answer him. Someone deep inside me that I didn't know suddenly possessed me. "Get undressed," I told him quietly. "I just want to look at you." When his body was at the mercy of my hands and my eyes, I longingly admired the force that offered itself to me. He looked me straight in the eyes. Since I didn't move, he lowered his eyes, blushed, and started to breathe more quickly. "What do you want?" he murmured.

I didn't answer. Suddenly this statue of a boy was at my feet. I can't describe it any other way. He hugged my thighs with his arms, and hid his face in my lap. I took hold of his neck and pushed his face into my stomach. I put his hands on my chest.

"You have girl's hands," I said with a laugh, although it wasn't true.

He showed me his palm: "Say it isn't true," he asked me. "Say it, say it."

It was always with this kind of trick that I got the better of him. His beauty was tumultuous, subject to change, somber one minute and then suddenly brilliant, depending on whether he was in a moment of melancholy or in the throes of pleasure.

Why did I think like that? No one can remember better than a boy who dreams of all that he's done and of all that he's loved. He only envisions the most essential. All his passions are simple ones, of which he remembers only the most perfect image. This is why I remember the smallest details of this story. All I needed was a moment of silence deep inside myself in order to see the shape of Gerard's fingers on the page of a book, or the blotch of ink on his cheek, the exact outline of his body under the sheets. I had the feeling that between the rest of the world and me there rose up a wall that went as high as the stars, isolating my cousin and me. Happiness was this protective wall.

The night came when my father and my uncle left for Paris. The house became paradise immediately thereafter. That night we slept in the barn. Taking our blankets with us, we explained to our cousin that it was too hot to sleep in our rooms, and that we'd be better off under the starry sky. She thought we were a little crazy, but didn't stand in our way.

The night that began looked as though it would never end. I left Gerard's arms only to throw myself back into them, like a swimmer who dives and resurfaces unceasingly. I became familiar with the ever-increasing swells of this ocean of pleasure, with its obscure restful depths. We stopped time in the space of just one night. We loved each other as if it was already too late, but that's how love sings its eternal swan song. As a human being, I lacked the language to express what I could not convey with mere words and caresses.

Around two o'clock in the morning, when the night was getting chilly, I realized that Gerard was crying. It happened when I bent my arm, which was under his neck, and I brushed his cheek. It was cold. He turned to hide his face in his arms. I grabbed his neck forcefully and made him reveal his face. He was having trouble breathing. I put my forehead against his face and his sobs broke against my skin. He was suffocating and wanted to escape from me. I held onto him more tightly. I was half-mad. His tears excited me. I desired his sudden unknown pain, and so I caressed him more deliberately. He pushed me away, so I slapped him. He couldn't fend off my blows, because I knew that I was the stronger one. I hit him. In the evening silence, the noise of my blows united us as if we'd been making love . . .

Night was almost over. Gerard was sleeping; I was dreaming. What was wrong with him? Neither my questions nor my caresses could convince him to tell me. "I love you. That's all," was all he would tell me. I think that in fact that *was* all. Loving someone is a kind of unhappiness. For two lovers, even a clear sky can seem like a stormy one. We had three whole days before our fathers were due to return. I was conscious of our approaching misfortune.

Gerard was sleeping. He was more beautiful than ever; in sleep he had found once more the tranquil face of a child. A little bit of drool linked him to his cradle, as if this connection that flowed from his body was the only thing that still held him to the earth. He slept, while tiredness kept me awake. He dreamed, and his dreams desired that my eyes remain open. For him, I was love personified. I didn't know what he wants when he slumbers. How many similar nights do I have to confront before the dawn! We were already unhappy. Our love was a nocturnal one. His night was too long, and I love Gerard too much.

My God, I want to die!

Part Two: Gerard's Story

I

After lunch, we left the house right away. We went along the path that led to the barn. As soon as we were far enough away that we couldn't be seen through the window, I took Pierre by the neck, put his head on my shoulder, and kissed him on the mouth. Pierre is the handsomest guy, and I can do exactly what I want with him. When I walk next to him, I always feel like I'm marching in a victorious army parade: he's so self-confident that he seems like a regiment of ten thousand men all by himself.

He's carved from a solid block of marble, a bit wider at the shoulders and a bit thicker in the thigh, but with a thin waist. It is as if in the middle of all this robust flesh, some contrast was needed. It took the form of an athletic suppleness in the waist, whose curvature lent his haunches an androgynous grace. He had a Romanesque head, blue eyes, and brown hair. I might seem the weaker of the two of us, but actually, I'm the brute. Pierre is almost always calm and composed. His hair, although carefully combed, falls in long locks on his temples and forehead.

I love to bring him to tears with a feigned indifference of which I have complete control. An instant later, however, I do everything so that he'll forget and forgive the way I've been treating him (for the last time, of course). This is how I retaliate against the way I feel for him, because I hate loving him. I feel like master and slave at the same time, which makes me doubly susceptible to the inconsistencies of power and submission, both of which are fragile. I love Pierre more than anyone else ever could. I could resist this love, or even give in to my urges to destroy it, but there comes a time when you can't do anything about what you feel.

So, I was in the middle of kissing Pierre. I felt a slight sigh of relaxation when he opened his mouth, and then later, after the mysterious touch of one face against another, a second breath, more forceful this time, that signaled his return to himself, his rediscovered freedom. I tried to kiss him at least ten different times. Without him saying a word, I embraced him and took him toward the river to the first place that we'd made love to each other. I found the exact spot without even looking for it. We lay down on the grass and fell asleep, pressed together so closely that even a blade of grass wouldn't have slid between us.

When we woke up, we both felt the desire to do it. I looked so intently at Pierre as he was about to cum that I was frightened. His approaching pleasure looked exactly like sudden pain, so much so that I would have thought he was dying except for his shining pupils between his half-closed lids and the groan that separated his lips. Then we both lost consciousness. Even though I hadn't stopped contemplating him, a black veil seemed to fall that suddenly obscured my view. Some time elapsed before I saw the tree that was sheltering us emerge from a glittering fog to recover its movement and its color. Pierre looked completely different now. His cheeks shone; love had swelled his lips. He had that insolent air of someone who'd recently cum.

It was seven o'clock before we decided to go home. The house was empty. We sat down in the living room, and Pierre started to flip haphazardly through some magazine or other. I didn't want him to just sit there, so I grabbed at the pages and knocked the thing from his hands until he got sick of my persistence, capitulated, and agreed to listen to me. Here's what I told him:

"Pierre, my friend, you sit here reading in front of me and it's bothering me. First of all, I have the right to more respect than that. Secondly, you're supposed to be keeping me company. Therefore, I condemn you to a penalty of two kisses . . ." I forced him to give me his mouth, because he wanted to resist my enforced pleasure. He didn't resist very strongly, so I soon had his lips. At that moment, my father, whom I hadn't heard coming, entered the room.

I got up incredibly quickly, and was subsequently reassured by his exclamation, "Oh, there you are!" He hadn't seen us.

"We're over here," I said. "We mere mortals were just sitting here, hoping for a visit from Mount Olympus." He didn't like my sarcastic tone. Instead of answering, he looked at me furiously.

I had a feeling that I knew what was behind this supposedly impromptu visit. A few days beforehand, I had stumbled into a conversation that our fathers were having with a few charitable souls, the sort of insignificant provincial types who are interested in money, status, scandal, and not much else. For them, money replaced beauty. They condemned us because we were only seventeen and were very handsome. Our love didn't represent anything in terms of money or prestige. All of these people were afraid of what they themselves weren't living in their sordid little lives, where love was something to be had in a four-poster bed with pink silk sheets. This is why they covered our love with the torrents of bile that ran in their veins in the place of blood.

From this conversation heard while eavesdropping from behind a door, I learned that my feelings for Pierre, as hidden, I had thought, as they were, were totally obvious to everyone else. Apparently our amorous glances said what our mouths didn't. Lovers like us are so filled with their dreams that their love unwittingly spurts from them like a fountain. Everyone around them is inadvertently drenched in it.

This was how our fathers were subjected to the charming commentaries of their charming friends who did their best to blacken my name so that even the night seemed luminous by comparison. Pierre was described as a young innocent led astray by a demon, despite his best intentions. I told him that I was flattered to have such observant enemies. Pierre was, however, worried. Several days passed before our fathers let on that they were watching us. As usual, we went to each other's rooms at night by climbing out the windows. Accordingly, our pleasure possessed a newfound intensity that is typical of activities performed under Damocles' sword.

It was the day after (perhaps provoked by my cheeky comment about them descending from on high) that our fathers decided to take the offensive. At the end of lunch, Pierre's father took him aside and asked him if he wouldn't like to spend a few days in Paris in order to sign me up for the bac and to buy me the volumes of Titus Livy that I needed for my studies. He also offered Pierre some tickets to a concert (a last-minute idea for a bribe, no doubt). Pierre dissembled, delayed, and finally defeated them; in two days, they'd go to Paris by themselves to take care of some urgent business. They reproachfully told us that *they* didn't have the luxury of three months of vacation. I took their insinuations in stride; I wasn't even tempted to respond. They couldn't get a rise out of me. My skin was thick enough so I did not worry about this sort of attack. Most of the time, I would prefer to avoid the sort of conflict where in the end, they'd resort to other, more violent types of punishment in order to get the better of me. My father just loved to demonstrate his authority.

The second offensive took place on the battlefield of the bathroom the next morning. My laziness was the target. I was naked, just getting out of the shower, still covered with water. I shook myself like a dog, sending droplets everywhere. Pierre, already dressed, was combing his hair in front of the mirror. My father, who absolutely never used this bathroom, entered suddenly. I am sufficiently beautiful that even my father can't help staring when he occasionally sees me naked. So, he stood there admiring me. Maybe he saw the image of his dead wife in the slender-waisted, white-skinned boy that I am. Pierre was also staring at me. His gaze flattered me and let me know that I was his—as he would be mine as soon as my father left. This, however, wasn't really the reason for what happened next. I hadn't moved. Water was beading on my chest, running down my stomach, along my thighs, and into the brown curls of my pubic hair. All of a sudden, my father gave a sort of strangled cry. Was his furor caused by feelings of ecstasy and desire that I had provoked in him?

"Get out, Pierre" he said. And then, "No. Why don't you stay?" He turned to me. "You. Get dressed instead of displaying yourself. You spend hours in the bathroom, staring in the mirror, having fun in the tub, while your books gather dust on the table. You just don't give a damn about anything, you useless brat. I have had enough. I'm sending you to summer school until your exam. Go. Pack your bags. Go, I said! Get out of here!" I didn't move a muscle. Pierre opened his mouth to say something. My father stopped him: "No. Keep quiet." And to me: "So, you're not going? Do you want me to help you?" I was as still as a statue. "You asked for it!" my father shouted.

Twisting my arm, he brought me to my knees and then slapped me in the face with the back of his hand. Before I realized what was happening, he took me across his knee. He beat the hell out of my ass in front of Pierre! The sound of his hand against my naked backside must have excited him. Afterward, Pierre claimed that he looked like he was going to have an orgasm, he was enjoying it so. I, however, was filled with shame by the sound of the blows. Although at my age, and in front of my cousin, I would have preferred that he hit me with his fists, I didn't struggle.

My father hit me hard and let his hand linger so that it would really hurt. It sounded as though he was applauding something. After about twenty smacks, I was overwhelmed with a burning sensation that spread into my thighs, climbed voluptuously into my lower back, and branched out into my side only to bloom, in a long painful caress, through my chest and into my nipples. Little by little, the blows became less violent. His hand hurt him, and he forgot his fury. He remained solemnly silent after this outburst, and then left the room apparently embarrassed to have delivered such a demeaning lesson mixed with a vague impropriety in front of my cousin. He never said another word about summer school.

Alone with Pierre, I looked at him. I would have made the punishment seem like a joke, but I was horrified to have been humiliated like that in front of him. One wrong word would have made me take my anger out on him. My father had done his best to make me seem less statuesque in Pierre's eyes. I had been transformed into a little brat who just needed to be spanked, only twelve years old instead of seventeen. I turned and looked in the mirror to see if I was red. My buttocks shone so provocatively that I felt my throat close and my head spin.

Pierre approached me, fell to the floor, and put his cool cheek against my burning flesh. You could see the outline of my father's fingers on my skin. He stayed that way for at least five minutes, hugging me tightly against him. He must have forgotten which cheek he was pressing against him, because all of a sudden, he pressed his lips to my buttocks. I was immediately transformed—from my head to my toes—into a giant kiss. The voluptuousness of this light touch overtook my entire body by the same paths through which the pain inflicted by my father had spread.

My father made no allusion to what had happened, which indicated that he and my uncle could only be planning some sort of joint maneuver.

Lunch played itself out like a classical tragedy. Pierre and I sat there silently, while our cousin alternated between being our guard and our confidante. Our fathers talked about everything except us all the way through dinner. This was the first act. When dessert was served, the subjects of conversation became more indirectly personal, but their attempts to provoke fell flat. Pierre continued to misunderstand their allusions on purpose. I played the same game, answering their provocations nonchalantly. Thunder continually rumbled in the distance, which seemed appropriate for the dramatic developments of act two. What we really needed to do was to get out of there. In the past we had usually been able to do this, thereby lowering the curtain on the third act. This was absolutely not possible today. They asked us to stay for an after-dinner coffee and even took the extraordinary step of offering us a couple of cigarettes. I hesitated and then accepted one. Pierre followed my lead. We were walking right into the lion's den, but I knew this and promised myself not to give up without a fight. Loaded small talk has always irritated me; I would have preferred an honest talking-to, during which I could have nodded and looked contrite at the appropriate moments, while thinking of other things. My father's sweet tone was too insincere not to conceal a trap. Isn't baiting a grass-covered pit with ripe fruit the way they catch elephants in the Congo? I wasn't dumb enough to be fooled by a few rhetorical flowers. They told us about their plans for October. Where would we like to go? Perhaps I should spend some time in England to learn

English? After all, it's the best way to learn a language. Unless Pierre wanted to go with me, Rome seemed like the perfect place for him to practice his Italian. He still had a year before he had to decide what he wanted to study at school. They proceeded with their all-too-obvious ruse in this manner. I really felt like applauding their performance, but I was supposed to be the antagonist in this drama, not the spectator.

Pierre told them that it would be better to think things over. He needed time to decide. In the meantime, he thought it might be better not to make any sudden changes in order to give me the best chance of passing my exam. Now here was a good performance! Narcissus himself couldn't have matched Pierre's rhetorical prowess. Now all we needed was the denouement, which I happily provided. I informed my father that Pierre and I would generously accept a year in Rome; it was exactly the sort of marvelous idea that only fathers could come up with, and would motivate me more than ever to succeed in October. I only had three weeks left until the exam, I told them, and therefore could honorifically retreat to study before throwing myself into yet another uphill march. If this had been a Shakespearean play, at this point the words "exit, stage right" would have appeared. This is, in fact, exactly what I did, before they could get over their amazement at my cheek.

What happened afterward is hard to describe. They told Pierre to let me know that they had solved all our problems: I would remain in Paris with them, while my cousin would take Pierre to Italy. This was announced in a tone that didn't invite any sort of reply. My father would play Burrhus to Pierre's father's Seneca, and they would take turns looking after me, the young Nero. Pierre, on the other hand, would retire to the home of some vestal virgin or other. The curtain fell; the play was over. They were quite proud of themselves, convinced as they were of their abilities to predict our futures.

The brilliant summer gave way to a gloomy September. Vacation was almost over. In a few days we wouldn't even be able to talk about our break except in the past: "Do you remember last summer when we . . . ?" Earlier in the summer happiness had come to our seemingly tranquil household, showing us its own beautiful face, dreaming with us, sleeping with us, and little by little, imperceptibly leaving us. We'd only realized it was going after it had already bid us farewell. It was too late: summer was over. Who could have given me the power to turn back the clock? My future looked rather dim. At seventeen you have the force, but not the means to fight. Ironically, you have the potential for almost anything—except love, that is.

At dawn the next morning, our fathers left for Paris in the car. They had papers to sign and their own lives to take care of. They weren't worried about leaving us alone together since it wasn't for very long. All of a sudden, their departure and my impatience for freedom gave me an idea: Pierre and I would also leave, but for good. Either that, or I would kill myself.

Maybe I was typical for my age, but the idea of death appealed to me. I was intrigued by its grandiose and romantic appearance. Interminable winters, incendiary blazes, its violent storms—everything that had the violent power of sudden and total destruction delighted me. The idea of a slow, peaceful death, on the other hand, disgusted me. I couldn't think of anything more boring than its autumnal hues of twilight melancholy and its sadly falling leaves. The nonchalance of the hours thickened my blood in the same way that it invaded the forest undergrowth with a slack and tepid rottenness. It made it swampy and faded, but filled with that sort of dark-colored vegetable precipitate whipped up into a fury by the winds of death. Real death—that is, winter—had the lively brilliance of a liquid gem. Waiting through fall, however, made death seem insipid and heavy. It seemed to disavow the very existence of springtime. I was born in the spring, during the time of the year when young men kill themselves. I hated October for being such a calm month. Yes, it is a red month, but of the sort of rusty red that has too much brown mixed in to evoke the richness of blood. For me, May was the cruelest month, the time of scarlet.

August was as hot, if not hotter, than May. Something in me was chilled, however. I longed for another spring. Pierre understood my impatience. He didn't like to wait, either. Autumn is just a sad and endless evening of waiting. We hung on to the last few days of our vacation, but in reality, it was already over. The September light had already extinguished the last night of August. September wasn't really the fall; it was worse. It was just a longing for fall. Soon we'd be counting the days, and then the hours, and then the last unlivable minutes. How I longed for the things that I imagined! I wanted to see the months that loomed ahead, to know the future where it concerned my love. The rest of the Earth could have disappeared, and I wouldn't have cared at all. Pierre was my universe.

For once, I decided to think things over before rushing ahead. Usually, this would have made me impatient. Instinct was my version of logic. This time, necessity made me look within myself. All the castles in the clouds that had been constructed by my imagination were only fun and games next to the wanderings of my spirit. Even the most gifted engineer would have been unable to dam the stream of my racing blood, the force of whose torrent was love's rage and dreams. They might as well have tried to dry up the sea. It would have been an easier task!

Pierre was discouraged, and his hopelessness was getting to me. Some other time, I would have started to joke. I would have dragged him to the bed and lavished my love on him in order to lighten his body of its burdens. Right now, I wanted him to sink into his fear, to feel the futility of his beating heart until he was nauseous. I wanted the coursing of his blood to pound louder and louder in his head until he threw himself into my arms, crying and ready to commit murder. I wanted to know if he believed that our love was worth the price of blood. I didn't have to wait long.

I was sleeping when our fathers left at daybreak the next day. The crunching of their footsteps on the gravel amplified by the stillness of the dawn woke me. I heard the wheels of the car roll out of the driveway and, as if on cue, an explosion of bird sounds as soon as the gate squeaked closed. All of this contrasted with the thunderous silence of only a moment before, which had rung with such intensity that you could almost feel it throb in your temples. Although our fathers' recent departure improved the morning's prospects, the silvery blue light of the morning left me feeling cold. Pierre was up, too, and stirred in my bed. We opened the door to between our rooms, so that he could reach his bed quickly in case footsteps on the stairs announced a surprise visit from my cousin. No one came, however, so we remained in bed, staring at the sky through the window. The car containing our fathers progressed down the road. We heard it for only a few seconds after it left the house, and then it was gone, supplanted by the sounds of nature. At last we were in love and alone.

We were alone, almost as if we were living alone together, two boys without any feminine complications between us. It was possible, not so much because of the weaknesses borne of dark feelings, but from a virile attachment forged of camaraderie and love. We were united in the ordinary minutes that comprise each day, inextricably linked by spending time together, experiencing things together, fighting and dreaming together. I expected too much from our isolation to be disappointed; I was sure that we would discover, by whatever means necessary, a way to save ourselves.

Three days. That wasn't very long, but it seemed an eternity to two boys who had decided to love each other freely. Thanks to the time we'd spent studying together and to all our free time, we had unwittingly managed to spend more and more time alone together. We weren't even trying to fulfill passion's demands. Then, as if this weren't enough, we lived at night while sleeping next to each other. We wanted not hours, but days to spend in the rapture of a life lived in common.

I watched Pierre eat, drink from a glass, open a book, rest. It was the simplest moments of our existence that brought me the most intense happiness.

At night, a mask of sweat painted my face. Pierre dried it, and watched over me while I slept. How many times did a strong instinctual feeling—the kind that is second only to purely animal impulses in the passionate way that they affect the heart—awaken me? I would open my eyes to find his staring at me, jealously guarding deep within them the treasure that was my slumber. I couldn't believe that we'd be old one day, but still would have laughed out loud had someone told me that we had no future.

We got out of bed at nine o'clock and left for town at ten. I asked Pierre to give me all the money he had, to which I added all that I found in my father's desk. I didn't have any of my own to add since I hadn't been given any since I'd failed the bac. My father was of the opinion that my school vacation was enough of a gift, and that I was the kind of boy who'd spend too much on his girlfriends anyway. Pierre had a moped, for which we stole some gas out of the garage. We still needed to buy a map and a couple of rucksacks, since it would be impossible to put our suitcases on the back of the bike. We were preparing our escape.

We didn't have to look very long in Amboise to find what we needed. By a stroke of luck, the first store we tried had exactly the kind of bags that we needed. In fact, they were exactly the sort of rustic backpack of which I'd been dreaming when I imagined us on the road. Just because we were running away didn't mean that we shouldn't do so in style. Beauty is always important, even in cases of desperation. I'd brought with me a bunch of books, which (to my complete delight) I was able to get rid of for a little bit of money at the bookstore, even though I could tell that the clerk didn't really think he'd be able to resell them himself. Charm was our ally, and helped us get exactly what we needed. Pierre sold his records back to the record store, under the pretext that he was tired of them. My presence in the store bothered the clerk enough, however, that he didn't suggest buying any new ones. We bought a hunting knife for Pierre, and made it back to the house in time for lunch. We still had some six thousand francs to our name, as well as a Swiss watch and a ring that we'd stolen from my father.

The afternoon flew by. We tried out the knife by cutting some branches off a small tree, which we then whittled down into swords for a duel that revealed us as the kids that (sometimes, at least) we still were. I whipped Pierre's wrist so hard that it started to bleed. This made him so furious that he started to beat me violently. I had a hard time fending him off, but I managed to break his sword just before he was going to hit me in the face. "A minute later, and I would have fucking killed you," he said. The blood had more or less stopped flowing, but the place where I had hit him had turned purple and started to swell. He beat me often enough that I was actually happy to have given him a taste of his medicine during one of our games. He didn't understand that I hadn't done it on purpose. He threw my cruelty in my face, indignant. How dare I do something like that to him!

Well, what about me? What if one night, when he was having fun slapping me in the face while we were making love, I rebelled and hit him back? I chased these images out of my head. It was true: love had made a coward out of me. In bed I willingly spread my boyish pride before his feet, like a cloak for him to walk on. This is why I was so insolent during the day.

We avoided each other until dinner. The joyous ambiance of the veranda, candlelit and surrounded by flowers as it was, cheered Pierre up. As soon as he smiled at me, I smiled back at him. It was a humid evening. Lightning flashed in the distance and was followed by the lugubrious sound of nearby thunder, but it still didn't break the oppressive quality of the air.

The fan kept messing up Pierre's hair. He compulsively passed his hand through it to smooth it back into place. My cousin told us horror stories, but as it wasn't yet dark, I didn't bother pretending to act scared. Much later in the evening, everyone said good night. Using the heat as an excuse, we told her that we preferred to sleep in the barn, where it was cooler. She told us to bring a blanket anyway, because it was sure to cool off, and because there was the possibility of a storm later on. We dragged our bedding to the barn, which was completely dark. I took off my clothes, and threw myself facedown, completely naked on the blanket that I had spread out on the hay. Pierre spread out next to me. As soon as I realized that he intended to go right to sleep, I was overcome with sadness. I fought back tears, but they surged from my heart into my throat each time I sighed or even took a breath. I began to cry because I felt so alone in the presence of the person whom I loved. At that precise moment, there was a loud thunderclap. Pierre woke up and instinctively protected himself from the night's wiles by grabbing hold of me. As he brushed against my face, he felt my tears.

"What's wrong, Gerard?" He insisted I tell him. When I resisted, he took my head and shook it. I remained silent. He raised himself up, tilted my head back, and tried to kiss me. I bit my lips. Furious with desire, he spread my legs and took my dick in his hands. I pushed him off me. Without letting go, he slapped me harder than he'd ever done before. My tears didn't stop him. He was surprised by my courage, but knew that deep down I didn't really care about the pain. If it had been a different kind of pain, he would have done his best to soothe it. This kind didn't bother him at all.

"What is wrong?" he repeated. "Why are you crying? Talk to me, please." But I sank into my solitude like a drowning man. He could plead with me, caress me, order me to tell him, but I wouldn't say a word. I liked the hot impatience expressed by his tears. Only when he asked me in a whisper, "What is wrong?" did I throw the reason for my suffering in his face: "I love you. That's all."

He didn't seem to understand. I knew that it was impossible to describe a pain that was comprised of too much happiness. Love is a kind of disaster.

Pierre could adore me. He could pursue me through the depths of sleep. He could want me like a person wants anybody that he finds attractive. He would never be able to have me if I simply kept my eyes closed and dreamed about the night, the wind in the garden, the melancholy of a lonely nocturnal stroll. There was a wall of flesh erected between us in which love took refuge.

Our feelings for each other couldn't have possible grown any stronger since they were already bearing down on us with all the violence of a storm. As the time passed, however, our love laid the foundation of its fortress, brick by white brick. With each punch I became more and more enslaved, even though I should have run from Pierre's violence. It is true that I was cruel enough myself to tolerate the blows. Maybe I was so cruel that I would have even liked to return them in kind. In fact, I was so superbly cruel that I wanted him to hit me for this very reason. Pierre loved to beat me. This insult increased my standing in his eyes because, according to him, you could only beat a real man. My strength found its pride and my body found its pleasure in his brutality. Even more than being hit on the ass, I liked the sound of blows on my shoulders and legs. Being hit here hurt more. I had to bite my fist not to cry out.

Pierre took his time beating my thighs, perhaps because he liked the way that they became hot and red and made him want to cum when he rubbed against them. With the first blows, I tried to focus only on the whistle of the belt as it flew through the air. I tried to count the seconds between each strike in order to forget the humiliating position I was in. Later, I tried to imagine myself in Pierre's place, with him at my mercy instead. I was he, and he was beneath my whip. This way I was able to give into the blows, to offer myself up to them. I stretched out my body so as to make it more available to the inscriptions that they were leaving in my flesh.

This went on for some time. When I had stopped even reacting to contact of the belt, Pierre stroked my shoulders and then my buttocks with his palms. Then he took the belt and struck me again. His breath erupted from his body just as if he had cum violently. I called him, called his body. I wanted to possess him. For him, however, there was only one possible ending: he had to enter inside me in order to possess me. His penis hurt atrociously. I bit his arm, which caused him to bite the back of my neck hard enough to draw blood. Little by little, my pleasure overcame his savagery to the point where, with a cry, he announced the flash of his pleasure. Eventually it was my turn; I took possession of him and subjected him to the same sort of violence.

Usually, I was able to ensnare him in the quicksand of my words. This was my way of fighting against what frightened me. Fear was my drama: I was afraid of getting older. It wasn't that I worried about losing the softness of my skin, the freshness of youth; I was afraid of what we'd become. I wasn't interested in what was happening around me. Society with all its games didn't mean anything, really. I was surrounded by it, but could only imagine connecting with it through a tube of sleeping pills, a sharp knife, or a leap from a high window. My life was really just a refusal of death. This is what gave my love value. Pierre knew this without me telling him. My words intoxicated him, so he begged me to remain calm. When I was calm, however, he became scared of my silence. This was why I was supposed to talk to Pierre about our passionate life together in the future while he hid life's abysses and death from me by throwing me into the depths of love.

Around three in the morning I fell asleep without even meaning to do so. Pierre remained awake, watching me. I had a dream that I hesitated to tell him about the next day because I didn't want to frighten him. I was under an apple tree on the side of a deserted road. My knees were covered in blood, which was streaming onto the tar. I was really hurt. I held Pierre's blood-streaked face in my hands. His eyes were closed. His mouth was shut. He was dead. I must have moved a lot during this nightmare, because Pierre tried to calm me down by stroking my face several times. When the torments of night were finally over and dawn appeared with the pale face of a young boy, we realized that twenty-four hours had already passed since our fathers had left. We had made up our minds: we'd wait until the last day to leave.

This wasn't some mythic love, even though it seemed like the power of our love was the stuff of legends. We were Tristan and Tristan, Romeo and Romeo, the lover and the loved. We were ready for anything; nothing could hurt us. Even though the future didn't seem to hold anything except the distress, poverty, and loneliness of a life lived on the lam, it looked rich and full of promise to us. Our eyes were so filled with the indefatigable élan of passion that I didn't want to be apart from Pierre one instant. Despite the night of worry that I had just endured, I knew that we were going to leave and be together forever. There was, however, something even deeper inside me that knew that if death was the only force powerful enough to separate those whom destiny had united in an embrace, like two sides of the same coin or the two faces of Janus depicted on the gates of war, then death was the only way that either of us would ever liberate our souls.

II

Blood had always fascinated me. Both life and pain depend upon its movement through the body. We think it the origin of our strength. We have made the color of blood the color of war. Love's weapons are stained with it, as if loving was really just another form of combat. All of the legendary stories of passion that have taken place over the centuries are splattered with it. I myself have scars from the blows of its dagger, and bruises from its deadly kisses. The heart, where we think that courage lodges and cries of tenderness hide, is only there to bleed blood dry of violence and to hold back its voiceless music.

One morning, just as Pierre had finished washing, I stood in front of the mirror combing my hair, or rather wrestling with my unruly curls. Daylight was streaming through the open window, casting dark shadows from a nearby tree on our naked bodies, as if trying to hide our nudity. I couldn't really make out my own image in the mirror, just as I wasn't really able to see Pierre's face when I tried to imagine it with my eyes closed. Each second reshaped my features: a sunny moment made them shine, whereas a cloudy one lent them a melancholy depth. "You seem like twenty different boys all at once," Pierre told me. "I'm not sure which one I prefer—maybe a little of all of them."

I thought that the mirror reflected someone irritating, whom I stared at unflinchingly. The dark circles around my eyes betrayed long sleepless nights. My cheeks, reddened from being bitten and kissed, accused Pierre of both violence and tenderness. Pierre was standing with his eyes half-closed under the steaming shower. His whole body glowed. I was jealous of his beauty, because in the desire of young men there is always the desire to possess the beauty of the one admired. He dried himself off. As he threw his wet towel onto the side of the tub, his open arms seemed to offer his body to my caresses. He put his hands on me and slid them down my sides, first one and then the other. He then put one hand on my shoulder and, steadying himself with it, leaned over and bit the brown disk of my nipple. I pushed him off. I went over to the chair onto which we'd thrown our clothes and felt around until I found the knife we'd bought together. Pierre watched me intently. We were too close for him not to understand immediately what was going to happen. All the Pierres that I had known flashed before my eyes, from the daydreaming kid leaning over his books to the anxious young man surprised by a flat tire whom I had seen one day while we were driving. I remembered his expression so clearly and with such tenderness that I could have traced the curve of his cheek, the incline of his neck, with the tip of my finger. The half-closed eyes that hid the shining sadness of his gaze reminded me of his brown head pressed against the bed pillow, which in turn evoked the slowly descending face that approached my own when he leaned over to kiss me on the mouth.

There were so many Pierres in the bathroom that it felt crowded. They had assembled there to watch us exchange our blood. I wanted to offer the most vulnerable part of myself. All my passion was encapsulated in the moment. It was just an image, but it seemed as though we would have devoured each other on the spot, if we could have actually done it. I always asked more of myself for the sake of Pierre's love. Pierre, for his part, tried to love me more fervently every single day, as well. The peculiarity of our friendship is that we were always pushing the boundaries. We lived so far beyond ourselves that a world so disinclined toward love couldn't possibly understand us. Slowly I realized that I wasn't some eighth wonder of the world; I stopped looking for perfection in everything around me. Instead I took pleasure in the sweet, ancient feelings of which most people are no longer conscious, but which still reside deep within our bodies. Despite these sensations, there was still worry in my heart. Was this the proof of real love? Does a lover need to be afraid in order to assure himself of his passion, or does his fever hide the fear of waking from his dream one day to discover himself alone in the desert of night?

For days on end, I couldn't stand the thought of sitting down to eat. Even the sight of food made me feel sick because I was so stuffed with love. Then there were endless nights of sleeplessness, when I forced myself to lie still so long that I started to get a cramp, just because I didn't want to wake Pierre. You could have offered me peace; I would have blindly and blissfully embraced torment instead. The pain of love made me feel more alive. Even if unhappiness trailed me like a shadow, love is the only reason there is. Everything that is grand and exciting in life exists for it, through it, and with it.

I went toward Pierre; he shivered. I had to stroke him for a moment with the palm of my hand—almost as if he were a dog—to calm him down. As soon as he had relaxed a little I touched his shoulder with the knife. All of our various selves that loved each other crowded around to watch. I could feel their shadowy presence in the immense room. Their faces were as still as their ethereal bodies, which were shrouded in regal purple. The palace was pitch-black, except for one sole torch burning behind me. Pierre was naked. I was naked. Shadows and a ghostly forest of young men surrounded us. A black marble vessel stood before us, waiting to receive our blood. It seemed the antithesis of our pale bodies, which stood out against the crimson gloom. The knife began to glisten. The dull thud of the leather sheath muted the sound of Pierre's hurried breath as it fell to the ground. I grabbed his arm.

Our chests collided. Pierre's mouth was half-open. The point of the knife hesitated almost imperceptibly as it sank painlessly into the resilient flesh of his shoulder. His flesh vomited a stream of red that snaked down over his muscles. My cousin's chest tensed and became hard. I threw myself upon his wound, drinking the blood, sucking this life-liquor of his heart with all my might. Pierre's blood was sweet and slightly salty. I became intoxicated as it filled my mouth. I became engorged with his warmth as I gulped it down. At last, I left this sweet spring of Pierre's blood. It was as if virile love had mysteriously annihilated itself through the body of its lover. Behind the blood ritual of this subterranean religion was the offering of a mother who gives of her own flesh so that her child can ingest and enjoy it. In our love, that of one young man for another, this same motherly love existed as if one of us was the other's child.

His blood quenched a thirst that neither his saliva nor his sperm would have sated. This thirst wasn't simply my body's desire; it was the desire to be Pierre's desire itself. Pierre was my dream; he was the incarnation of a seventeen-year-old heart. He was joy, friendship until death, the loneliness of two lovers in a garden pressed against a wall, surrounded by the night. He was the sadness of one boy holding the other, their need for each other. All of this was contained in Pierre's blood. Over the years our varied interests and individual friendships had separated us. Blood united us now with its impatient ardor. Pierre was everywhere that I was. Pierre was more than just one person: we didn't know anymore where exactly my soul stopped and his began. Each day, I learned to live as him. We became so similar that, even though we didn't really look anything alike, people mistook us for each other because love had given us the same face. With his blood in my mouth, I went beyond mere love and attained an apex. I was Pierre transcended. Our friendship cast off all the worldly grime in which most people were content to wallow. In our bodies we felt a furious passion for life, while our hearts were filled with the sweetness of death.

I hadn't made any promises or sworn any oath, but something stronger than any vow bound me permanently to this man. It was this unarticulated attachment that made us awkward around each other—even in bed, at night, when we told each other, "I love you." We kept running into reality, like a bird that tries and tries again to fly through a closed window. Pierre's face was my isolation. An unknown force pushed me toward him. Destiny had shuffled the deck and had allowed the two of us to pick but one card: the ace of hearts, or perhaps the ace of blood, which hid our shared future. Our future! It seemed to me like some long nocturnal odyssey.

Loving Pierre made me a better person. Being next to him made me aware of the existence of a God in whom I had refused to believe until now. I could see Him watching me, through Pierre's eyes, as I slowly came closer to know Him through the storms of passion and the lulls of tenderness. I humbly implored Him, because all infinity was His and He had made us realize this, to join us with a word stronger than those written on the gates of hell: "ALWAYS." For me, always was an eternal now.

I lacked the calm assurance of happiness. My feelings were too violent to make the person whom I loved happy, even though all of my desires depended on it. I discovered a new horizon every day; where there had once been clouds was now clear sky. If we had wanted to create a holy order for all of the reflections of ourselves that had witnessed our love, we wouldn't have created a Theban legion, but rather a round table, where each of the knights was the other's equal.

Pierre took his turn making me bleed. He grabbed my arm, and I felt his mouth on the wound. The same thoughts kept running through my head: *Pierre loves me. Pierre lives.* I put my forehead on his shoulder, my eyes closed.

It was then that all the little notes that love scribbles appeared before my eyes, as if my hand had been guided by its own. I remembered one letter in particular, one that I had written while waiting for Pierre, when I suddenly felt very alone and afraid that he would be taken from me:

> My Pierrot,
> I am jealous of the air that you breathe. I hate the light that fondles you in front of me. I can't tell you how much I love you and how much I want you.
> —Gerard

Everything that we wrote each other stayed inside us, articulated only through the physical expressions of our pleasure. It wasn't that we couldn't translate our secrets into words, but rather that we were afraid of what we would have said. These words were more than love. They were a kind of affection that strove to transcend human chronology to attain eternity.

Pierre's love was inherently jealous. I had completely forgotten my past; only his name stayed in my head. The other people I had known disappeared little by little until they were no more. In fact, I would have willingly destroyed the memory of everyone I had ever known before him, if this simple desire hadn't already made them dead for me.

Up to this point, love had really only satisfied my taste for violence. My cousin had made me discover its tenderness. During a moment of sleepiness spent next to him, or during our unconscious embrace while asleep, I would have stoically refused the most excessive pleasure and endured the worst pains. I had lost all my friends because Pierre became irritated with me if I so much looked at another boy. If I was unfriendly, he also reproached me for that. I didn't know what to do. My love had grown so that Pierre couldn't ignore the fact that only he existed for me. All the compliments that people paid me, all the desiring eyes that had followed me over the years, had given me plenty of self-confidence. This armor became useless the first time that Pierre kissed me. As much I had enjoyed being looked at in the past, it bothered me now. I only wanted to be seen by his eyes. I didn't want him to find anyone else like me. The hours that we spent together had to be his entire existence. When I thought about myself, it was always in the past tense, as if I were dead. In this way, I was just following the dark progression from thinking depressive thoughts to imagining my death. Ten times I lived my suicide. I worked everything out to the smallest detail in my dreams. It would happen at night in Paris, although I'm not sure why I thought this. I imagined myself alone in a dark room, waiting for Pierre. Impatience was a facet of my passion, which made each second that passed seem like the stab of a knife.

He didn't come, and time was suffocating me. I was holding a big glass of liquid in my hand, which I brought to my lips. As soon as I took the first sip, I knew that the drug it contained would kill me. I drained the glass nevertheless. By the time Pierre finally arrived, I was already beginning to die. He didn't understand what had happened right away, at least not until the sweat shone so on my pale body that it looked as though I had bathed in melted silver. He spread me out on the ground. I doubled up in agony, trying to breathe. At other times, I imagined other ends for myself, but the story always finished with me dying at the feet of my cousin . . .

I didn't want to see any further. Survivor's guilt would be worse than death, so I promised myself that neither Pierre nor I would know it. Lovers that can tolerate posthumous living aren't really in love, since the one who remains is left with just half of a conversation, half of an amorous gaze, half of a desire, half of an irreplaceable body. He can only look at the stars through half an eye, while caressing himself and telling himself that night approaches. I often conjured up the scene of my death. Pierre couldn't understand why I would suddenly fall sullenly silent.

Several times I had taken him for a walk through the garden in the evening. We would leave the house silently, our shoes in our hands, wearing only jeans that we took off as soon as we were beneath the trees. Even when it was humid out, the air seemed to caress our flesh voluptuously. We touched each other while we walked toward the river into which we then threw ourselves. I always chose evenings when the moon was high in the sky for our walks because Pierre looked like an ivory statue in its icy light. If we swam on top of the water, the moonbeams illuminated our bodies and made us glow. The wind dried us.

While we were still wet, we would wrestle, which would always end up as a confused embrace. I remember Pierre's back, flat against a tree while his wet thighs slid between my hands. Pierre's neck seemed divided in two by a deep groove that continued down his back.

Pierre appreciated my vigor, whereas I was intent on pleasure. I made him stretch out in order to get to know the smallest detours of his lovely valleys. He hid his face between his hands. When I climbed on top of him it was no longer a landscape of love over which I flew, but rather a giant bird of flesh that took me on its wings to soar above the mortal storms and into the silence. I was a meek and loving being who was only transformed into a wild beast through inattention.

I always fell back to my lonely Earth. I knew that we would have to earn money for our life together, and therefore that we wouldn't be able to remain alone forever. This offended and annoyed me. When other people got to share Pierre with me, even through simple proximity, I had to stop myself from holding his hand. It was so unfair that I couldn't put my head against his and talk about love! This made me suffer terribly. Invisible torments ravaged my heart, which Pierre could see. He asked me what was the matter, but what could I say except that I loved him?

I love him. This phrase was irreplaceable. After only a month of our vacation, it seemed ridiculous whenever I started to say it. As soon as it surged from my mouth, however, it was reimbued with its spring-like purity. Love taught me the marvelous language that turns every lover into a poet. Sometimes a flash of joy would light up my night. Just as nocturnal bolts of lightning illuminate the details of the ground below with an uncanny clarity so intense that out of the dark disorder appears the vast horizon, so did this stroke of brilliance in me reveal the violent reality of my passion. This revelation didn't last long. These mutations of feeling, which seemed as variable and as volatile as lava, made me suffer so much that I was unable to live in the present moment.

We were completely insouciant of time. Only the color of the sky told us that hours were passing. The days all seemed alike. We decided to put our faith in the sun's promises, to believe in the pulpy sweetness of the night. Dawn's cold grip on our bodies marked the passing of another night as it offered up their secrets to the red morning light. Love was our calendar; we celebrated the body's holidays and the soul's seasons. With the delight of youth, we gorged ourselves on pleasure, hurrying through the evenings in order to have longer nights. Only the sun had seen us swollen with joy, and had kissed our naked bodies with its murderous lips.

The fact that Pierre belonged to me made me feel like a rich man. I knew what it was to be wealthy beyond my wildest dreams because of the opulence that lived in the body of this boy. Even though I now had everything that I had ever desired, I was still aware of how little it would take to find myself empty-handed: even one lonely afternoon, shut up in my room by myself, would do it. I didn't know how to keep Pierre during his absence. My head was filled with the futile sound of blood coursing through my temples as if going up a gigantic staircase. Since I was so sensual, for me my cousin was above all a being of flesh; his soul had a mouth and thighs that smelled like those of a young male. All the rest of him emanated from there.

When he moved to drink my blood, Pierre sacrificed himself as I had sacrificed myself. He wanted to be Gerard. He built his future on a past that was half mine and half his, double and unique like twins. We didn't even need to look at each other in order to know exactly what the other was doing. We were marionettes whose puppeteer was love. And then, these fleshy dolls escaped their master to become intelligent machines who clamored not only for movements dictated by pleasure, but also for extraordinary souls. We wanted more than banal feelings, more than a body addicted to mere sensation. We wanted to become so incredible that men would call us gods, at which point we would go even farther to attain, with childlike steps, the highest summits of ecstasy.

Pierre got up, his lips slightly reddened by the blood that he had been drinking. We stood still for a moment, overwhelmed by what we'd been doing. The cuts were already closed. Our love was already consecrated.

At last we awoke. The ceiling was sunlit, and a tree threw the shadows of its branches on the window. I looked around and saw that the assemblage of young men dressed in regal purple who had witnessed our ceremony had disappeared.

As if to make us eternal captives for having tried to steal its treasures, memory closed the heavy doors of its prison upon us. I was suddenly confronted with all of life's torments. Among these was the insurmountable anxiety provoked by the passage of time. All of a sudden I knew the endless distress of a boy who holds another in his heart. I could sense the end of the lovers' stroll, the last waltz, the parting glance. A torrent of worry rushed over me like the vigorous arm of a river of solitude whose sadness overruns the eroding shores of desire.

I was well aware that romantic sentiments were out of fashion. Heartfelt emotion was naive kitsch. I suppose that if I could have been more blasé about the whole thing, it would have seemed more natural and would have hidden our happiness. Loving another boy would have almost looked normal; we would have seemed like everybody else. In their eyes, however, any love that refused to inhabit their world was not normal. Our love was like that of all the historic lovers who have rejected virtue, family, and history as if they were exterior accidents. Whether in Verona or Rimini, or in this case, near Amboise, our dreams were the same.

Our love was night. It was the fresh cheek of dawn, the revelries of our joyous flesh. Other people could abandon their fickle desires, could follow their whims. I had deliberately chosen the narrowest path, on either side of which yawned an abyss.

I would fight to keep Pierre for me and for me alone.

III

The property next to ours was the fiefdom of a family of bankers. It is a bit of an understatement to say that I hated them. Three sons and a daughter were the principal crop of this farm of family values and family crests. The first time that I met our summer neighbors was at the tennis club. Being the best player, I spent the whole afternoon trouncing them, one after the other. Although it was a hot day, the whore that secretly exists in me (and, in fact, in every man, if he's the least bit handsome) was the real reason that I took off my shirt that afternoon.

I was the focus of everyone's attention. Pierre was both delighted and disappointed by my performance. The force behind my smashes and the way that I stayed in the center of the court confounded him and everyone else. I wasn't a gracious winner, which made the guys start to hate me and my lack of modesty, even though they admired my muscular legs and all the rest of me at the same time. After I had taken off my tennis clothes and was in my underwear in the locker room, one of them offered to towel me off. The red clay of the court had reddened my socks and calves. With my towel, he scrubbed my shoulders, my lower back, and then after a moment of hesitation, the backs of my thighs. I pretended not to notice anything and he ventured a bit further. Pierre paced back and forth in front of the sink. To the other boys, it looked like Philippe Decazes was helping me out; to the two of us, it felt like he was caressing me. Our complicity lasted the whole trip back, him at the wheel of his car and me seated beside him. Pierre returned to the house on the back of his sister's moped. The other two brothers returned in their own vehicle. They thought we'd just spent a fun afternoon together and so invited us back for the next day. That evening I swore to Pierre that I'd never give into the thrill of a sexual conquest again. To make it up to him, I let him do what he wanted to me.

Philippe Decazes came to get us the next day. We were alone in the garage for a few minutes while Pierre returned to his room to get the key to his padlock. The boy tried to flirt with me, pulled me toward him, and just at the moment when he thought he was going to kiss me, received a mouth full of an oily rag that I had picked up from the floor. The rest of the evening was a bit gloomy: Pierre didn't say a word, and Philippe stared at the ground silently. As for the others, I captivated them by acting like a Young Turk. We ate dinner in an inn on the banks of the Loire. After we had finished, Philippe proposed a race home with different routes depending on the type of transportation, so that even the moped would have a chance of winning. The last people to arrive would have to buy alcohol for everyone else.

Under the pretext that his old Delahaye sedan had the fastest motor, Philippe chose the most deserted and circuitous route of all for the two of us. Then, in the middle of our trip, he pretended to have a breakdown. I told him that although he might have enough cash to afford to be last on purpose, I was broke and that there was no way I was going to pay for everybody. I told him that I wouldn't ask Pierre to loan me the money, either. He drew near me: "I'll give you the money . . . and even more than that, if you want." His arm was around my neck. Although we were fairly well matched in strength, I had already had too much to drink to defend myself properly and didn't do a very good job holding my ground. Philippe pushed me onto the reclining car seat, put his arms around me, and forced my lips open with his own. He told me how handsome I was and how rich he was. He said he had his own apartment in Paris and that he could take care of me. When he undid my belt, I bit him on the lips. He finally managed to pull down my jeans, at which point I drunkenly gave in to pleasure. I stopped fighting and grabbed him by the ears, helping his violent caresses. We were a bit cramped and my jeans were tight around my ankles so I took them off completely. As I was already half standing up, I bent Philippe over and sat down on his face. His profile spread my cheeks. I could feel his hot breath and his nose, which was smashed under my weight. His lips opened for my pleasure. I grabbed onto his neck from above and pressed down on him even harder. His tongue violated me. The feeling was at first so unbearable that it stimulated a network of nerves so violently that I felt it all the way to my nipples. Then, when his saliva had lubricated my muscles and his tongue-turned-dick had forced me to give in, I gave myself up to his touch that was insinuating itself into my entire body. . . . I groaned in spite of myself. The night was warm, and my body was burning as if I had just emerged from a bath of ice. I wanted to murmur, "Go on, Pierre, go on," as I had next to the pond, and to cry out to the night, to the moon, "I love you." Summer isn't exactly a tender season, and yet, at dusk everything around us seemed softened. I loved the hour of the day when the light beneath the willows becomes blurred. At that moment next to the pond, when we were holding each other, naked, just before going home, I could tell that all of nature was looking at us; we were the fruits of its living dream. . . . The beeches and the oaks, our mute and massive brothers, didn't move a leaf. Blood gently invaded our bodies, which are pressed together against the background of the trees and the dying lights on the water. A profound joy opened its doors deep down in our flesh . . .

With his two hands, Philippe pushed my thighs apart in order to make me more available for his feast. I was devoured by an insidious pleasure whose movement transformed me into an endless spiral. These sensations could have turned me into a girl. I was, however, made only more virile by them, because it was my strength that was inspiring this homage. Besides, the man in me was enjoying the passive luxury of being serviced. It took another boy to transform Philippe's threat of rape (a violation that was really more mental than physical) into an apotheosis of maleness.

I don't know how long this had gone on when I was suddenly overwhelmed with fury. Drops of sweat ran into my mouth. I was coated with Philippe's saliva. I touched his face, which had suddenly stopped touching me, even though my body was still invaded. My fingers ran through his hair. When I felt his features, I was suddenly reminded that he wasn't Pierre. It was as if I someone had thrown cold water in my face; suddenly I was completely sober.

I stood up. He thought that it was to give him a better angle and pulled me back down on the seat. I smashed my fist into him and sent him flying against the car door. Without waiting for him to respond, I threw myself on him and continued to hit him. I punched him in the face. He was blinded and couldn't see me to strike back. At last I got out of the car and, standing against it, pulled him through the window by the back of the neck. I started to slap him in the face with absolutely no thought of self-control. When he stopped struggling, I threw him back onto the car seat and shut the door that he had half-opened. I put on my jeans and started to walk home. There was no one on the road; Philippe had chosen the route well. The moon was high in a sky filled with clouds too pale and thin to dull its light as they passed before it. They seemed to run from one end of the sky to the other, with what almost seemed at times to be strange cries, although these must have come from some nocturnal bird or other.

As soon as I had walked through the door to the house, I threw myself into the tub without turning on the light or even getting undressed. I wanted to drown myself in order not to smell the odor of Philippe's hands on my skin. I scrubbed my body with such vigor that my thighs became chafed. I wished that my ass were bleeding so that the pain of that wound would have overtaken his saliva and the feelings of pleasure that remained there. Philippe's mouth was, however, still the master; only Pierre's would be able to usurp it. Pierre had waited for us for quite awhile, before eventually deciding we got lost on purpose. He came back to the house after I did, and somehow knew to look for me in the bathroom. The tears that welled up in his eyes, which I had the chance to see before he turned away, were tears of joy, not anger. I couldn't endure any more that evening, and fell asleep with Pierre on top of me.

I knew, of course, the Decazes were going to get revenge. My massacre of their birds and our mutually affected politeness in front of our parents took my insolence and their rage to new heights. In fact, my impertinence surrounded me like a halo. They could sense this and wanted to have me, if only for an hour, in their hands. The opportunity soon presented itself, since treachery was their best weapon.

Without thinking, Pierre had mentioned in front of them that he was going into town to buy some records. He was gone all afternoon. They knew that they'd find me in the barn. Philippe Decazes went looking for me there, although he pretended that he just wanted to talk to Pierre. Before I even had the chance to realize what they were doing, I had been bound and gagged, thrown in a feedbag, and taken to their domain. In addition to the three Decazes boys, there were two other boys whom I had haughtily ignored often enough to make them want to smash my face in. At least, this is what I thought they wanted to do: in reality, it was much worse. When they let me out of the sack and stood me up, I saw that we were in the tower of the dovecote. On a table in the corner of the room, two riding whips and some rope were waiting for me.

One of the boys approached me and undid my shirt. He pulled it over my head and down over my wrists, which were tied together. Since I hadn't resisted at all up to now, he put his hand on my belt. I don't know how I managed to free myself, but I brought one fist up and punched him in the chin. There were five of them, so my resistance was as brief as it was futile. Another pair of hands pulled down my pants and underwear. They tied me to one of the pillars that held up the ceiling and took turns whipping me with the crop. I bit the inside of my mouth so as not to cry out. As my mouth was filled with blood, I was sufficiently distracted by the pain to make them realize that they weren't going to get any pleas for pity from me. They undid the ropes and I fell on the floor, stunned. I don't know exactly what happened after that, although I do remember that a while later, the weight of a body and a pain in my lower back made me try to stand up. The boy who was having his way with me pushed me back down onto the ground. Although I did everything I could not to show my disgust, I vomited. Those who hadn't yet had me did so covered in puke. This is how they took their revenge. After they were finished, they let me have a little water in order to clean myself up, and then took me back to the edge of our garden, encircling me silently all the way there. One of them threw my shirt in my face and pushed me onto our property.

When Pierre got back, he understood right away what had happened. In order to prove to me that I hadn't fallen in his eyes, he told me how much he hated them. He didn't just talk about the kind of irrational aversion that I had for the Decazes, but of his gut-wrenching hate for them, the kind of profound hatred that is the equal and opposite of admiration and love. Pierre claimed that people always liked me at first, but maintained that in no time I knew how to transform their affection into violent fantasies and then acts, almost without trying. Lively, but dull, their rage was more rancor than jealousy. Our neighbors had thought their conquest would be easy. They went so far that even the smallest refusal seemed like a grave insult.

For these little bean-counting bankers, besting me was not a game, but a business deal. They had designs on me, and demanded that I assume the role of their chattel. All these problems were the result of my shape, I knew. My face and my ass were my enemies. I could have added my need for pleasure to this list, if one considered this need some sort of inexorable force that motivated my behavior. I needed to cum as other people need to eat and sleep, which was why I was often orgasmically happy. A secret melancholy would reemerge only later, when for no reason I felt unsatisfied. I wanted to seem blasé, as if fulfilled by a life already saturated with adventure. I was one of those teenagers who were simultaneously delirious with enthusiasm and starving for pleasure. This is why the hate of which Pierre spoke had acted on my body with brutal gestures that, although they are camouflaged beneath the subterfuge of battle, are really acts of love. Even though I had already fainted, other more tender gestures had occurred during this violence. Perhaps because they had taken turns with me in front of one another, the only time that they could show me that they loved me was in the midst of their rage to satisfy themselves.

I didn't have the courage to explain all this to Pierre. He begged me to forget and not to do anything desperate. I was just a teenager. I spent the night pressed against his shoulder. In this sleepless night, I was certain that paradise was nothing other than a long night of love next to the being whose heart is the closest to our own.

I crossed paths with Michel Decazes two days later in town. He hesitated a moment, and then came toward me. We chatted in a friendly manner, as if nothing had happened. The complete lack of malice in my voice really caught him off guard. He was more upset than he would have been had I avoided him. His behavior in the pigeon house was still between us, however, since he had encouraged his brothers and had even taken his turn with me. His attitude revealed something that his mouth was trying to hide. In order for him to approach me, he had to be hiding something. After a few pleasantries about the hot weather, he said abruptly while looking me straight in the eye:

"I'm in love."

I received his avowal like a cruel caress. I turned red. How dare he tell me that he loved me in the middle of the street? Sure, I was used to this kind of admission, but usually not in the middle of some small talk about the weather (even though this kind of chitchat often conceals declarations of love). I pretended not to understand him.

"In love? How cute: a summer romance."

"Romantic or not, I'm in love, and you can help me."

"Me help you? What do you want me to do, sleep with someone for you?"

I wanted him to feel confused so that he would be forced to say what my body was already sure he meant. The body isn't always the heart's rival, however. This is why he was embarrassed by his half-admitted desires. His elusiveness explained why it was now his turn to blush. I waited, anticipating the pleasure of acting surprised when he at last named me as the object of his love.

You're in love with me? I would exclaim innocently. First I would act shocked, then angry, and finally, cruel.

"And who is it exactly that's making your heart flutter, if I may ask?"

"Pierre. I'm in love with Pierre."

His words came as such a surprise that it felt as if someone had punched me in the stomach. At any rate, this kid had no idea about how I felt about Pierre, and how he felt about me. I tried to understand. What exactly did he want from me? He was looking at me too severely not to have some trick up his sleeve.

"What are you up to this afternoon?" I asked him nonchalantly.

"Nothing, yet. I thought maybe we could go for a swim together. I've got my car, so we can drive to the Loire."

He was grasping at straws. In the moments of silence, between his desperate words, he was incredibly handsome. So, I said, cattily:

"Well, I'd better ask Pierre."

"You're worried that I'll get in your way."

"What are you talking about?"

"Hey, I know that he likes you . . . a lot."

"Yeah, a lot. I like him . . ."

I don't know why I didn't qualify my feeling with any adverb. All of a sudden, the sun emerged from behind a cloud and beat down on us. I guessed that I would have had to admit my love for Pierre to someone else, in fact to the exact person from whom I most wanted to hide it. Michel made a move that only guys, even when they hate each other, dare make toward another. He stuck out his hand for me to shake it.

That afternoon he took us in his car toward Langeais on one of those roads that is so pretty and so deserted that it feels as if you are happily driving toward some new world. I hadn't said anything to Pierre about what had happened earlier. We parked the car in a meadow and went toward the riverbank to sit down on some large flat stones. There was a reflective shimmer around the sandbanks. The heat made the beech trees on the island in the middle of the river seem to waver. Huge white clouds stretched out from one side of the horizon to the other, lying on the earth the way one lover lies on top of another. Pierre grabbed my neck and wrestled with me in a way that made it clear to Michel that it wasn't two friends, but two lovers he'd invited to go swimming. We were two lovers engaging in the kind of combat that is a prelude to love. Without realizing it, we must have really made him suffer.

Michel's brothers really held it against him for going out with us. He came more often, stayed longer, and left with the sadness of a confidant who can't help but watch. Now there was someone with whom I could talk about Pierre. Michel always listened to what I had to say with a seriousness that shouldn't have tricked me so easily. I told him everything, and everything I told him wounded him. Once, I asked him why he preferred Pierre to me. His answer told me something I would rather not have known:

"To you? You're the kind of person people want, not the kind they love."

As a result, I acted differently for a little while. All of a sudden, I preferred being alone. Pierre looked for me, but I wasn't there. His caresses hurt me. He had an idea that Michel had something to do with what was going on. One evening he told me that he could see that Michel and I were in love with each other, but that he didn't care. He just wished we'd told him. Then he burst into tears. I threw myself at his knees, and told him that no, it was Michel who was in love with him. I explained my sadness, my anxiety before this pain that, without even wanting to, I had let grow, even though I knew that it might somehow eventually be my downfall. Pierre became happy again. He didn't give a damn about Michel. He had thought that I didn't love him anymore, which made him feel like nothing. Now, none of that mattered!

Michel suffered even more during the days that followed. He eventually stopped coming at all, more or less at the same time that our fathers returned from Paris. This sped things up: he had been a big help to us without even realizing it. Thus love drives out friendship in much the same way that a usurper allows his followers to approach his throne, only so he can exterminate his rivals more easily.

Pierre had asked me to come find him in the grounds the same day that Michel decided not to come again. I was a little bit late leaving the house. When I arrived at the pond, everything was quiet. A heron stalked fish tranquilly. I called Pierre's name. No one responded, except for an ironic-sounding echo that threw my nervous tone back into my face. I didn't know what I was worried about. An accident? Or maybe something even worse? Not for a second did it cross my mind that Pierre was hiding so that he could watch me. The heavy flap of the heron's wings above the water made me decide to look among the bushes and reeds, but they were too dense for me to find my cousin. I started to feel sick.

I had often suffered during my childhood because I never had enough money to do what I wanted. It also hurt to be constantly misunderstood by the other boys, which happened more and more often as we started to mature. Even the desires that I provoked in others, but didn't share, gave me pain. I had known the isolation that a rebel feels when I was only fifteen because my dreams had shown me a world into which only I fit. Now, for the first time, I suffered because of desire. Unfulfilled, I could feel the ache of the word in my unkissed mouth and empty arms.

It was a completely hopeless pain. I wanted Pierre; I wanted him to be here now. The gloomy lake of silence refused to reflect the only image I wanted to see. Its immense surface remained untroubled, despite my calls to Pierre. Without him, life was hell. The craziest ideas kept popping into my head; first I imagined that Pierre didn't find me attractive anymore, and in fact was trying to avoid me. Going over things in my head made the smallest incidents take on dramatic proportions. Love was having a field day with my heart. The certainty that Pierre hadn't waited for me drove me to the barn like a wounded animal looking for refuge.

Then Pierre arrived and, to make a long story short, our bodies made up.

At dinnertime, we were surprised to find Michel, accompanied by his sister, talking to our cousin. He wanted to invite us to a surprise party at his house tomorrow. We promised to come. Since there were going to be a lot of people there, he took us aside and asked us to leave any grudge we might still hold at home. It would be best to arrive rather late, he said, after the wet blankets and the wallflowers had already left the party. We were supposed to go masked and in costume, so arriving late would also give us the chance to make a really grand entrance. Michel gave us some masks to wear, and his sister even offered to drive us into town so that we could all go to a thrift shop to find some costumes.

She picked us up the next morning. Pierre decided to dress like a Florentine prince after finding a laced doublet and a billowy shirt. He completed the look with some tights that stuck to him like a second skin. After weighing the options, I decided that the velvet mask would be my only disguise. I'd just put on some polo shirt and dark trousers; I didn't really care what I wore. The only thing that mattered to me was to leave the party as quickly as possible so that I could stretch out on the bed and be ready to receive the one I loved. For some reason, it felt as if my days were numbered, and as if I just didn't have time for parties anymore.

IV

"Pierre! There was that minute, that minute that had gotten away from me, that minute that was gone forever, during which nothing else in the world could be compared to the beauty of your face. There was your tenderness, your sweetness, your charm. I started to realize that for me, time was actually a dimension of you. You filled space and your body was my domain. Little by little, I succumbed to everyday worries. I stopped thinking of you as a brother, and started worrying about you as the lover on whom my whole future was staked. There was a long road ahead of us. I was counting on you, and hoped you felt the same sense of necessity. Necessity is, after all, the ancient name for fate! We were going to leave in less than a day now. In a couple of hours the party would take place. In a couple of minutes, we'd start getting ready. In one day's time, however, our future would stretch before us like a winding road around whose bends, strangely, I could not see . . .

"I was madly in love. Any idea that didn't have you at its heart wouldn't stay in my head. I imagined everything through you. Only when you spoke of me or to me did I exist. I really had to concentrate to remember even the recent past. I even believed that you had been the beginning of all desire for me. I renounced all those meaningless loves I had known before. What did it matter if I had let my body be used? All school kids are like that. This burden of love had deepened my gaze, laden my smile with bitterness and given my body a satisfaction afforded only by pleasure. I didn't really feel as though I had been enslaved, but I lost all will as soon as I showed you that I would love you . . ."

This was the way that I always talked, silently and inside myself, to Pierre. It was as if I were he, as if I had reproduced myself so that during the hours when we were apart there was another part of me to replace him inside myself. I waited for him, spread out on the bed, talking to him as if he were there. That morning, he had said something mean to me as he had stood in the mirror fooling with his hair for what seemed like more than an hour. Laughingly I had told him that he was worse than a girl; he had looked at me with an expression that made me feel ashamed. His eyes shone. Their lashes intensified the effect. His half-open mouth was calling mine. He was surpassing even his own beauty. And then, all of a sudden, he stopped being this dazzling god and resumed being his merely handsome self. This heavenly moment had passed. The fleeting impressions that are the fireworks of life always vanish as soon as they light up the night sky: like the powerful legs of a cyclist glimpsed so briefly that desire is mixed with regret, which in turn are both mixed with frustration at the impossibility of seeing them again; or like a ray of sun shining in a guy's hair; or the pure smile of a boy seen ever so briefly when he thinks no one is looking at him. All scenes of beauty are like this. The alacrity with which they disappear is the very essence of their charm. At age sixteen, a person dreams; at twenty, he dies of desire.

Attitudes are really important to young people. Everything presented me with an opportunity for effect. I continually threw myself into extreme situations in order to create trouble, and to make Pierre worry. He was no dummy, and so recognized and rejected my ploys for what they were. When I became entangled in my own provocations, Pierre would say coldly, "Stop acting like an idiot." Sometimes, however, he was wrong, and mistook one pose for another. Copping an attitude is sometimes the only way for a teenager to hide the weak parts of himself.

Once I went to London with my uncle, who had some business with an insurance agent. The firm was large and important, and so occupied a whole building by itself. There was an elevator to spare clients from having to climb the mountainous stairs that we took to the fifth floor. I had just turned fourteen. A young elevator attendant opened the doors for us and ran the machine. His friendly air, curly hair, and tight-fitting blue uniform with gold buttons totally overwhelmed me. I fell for him immediately. I wouldn't stop looking at him, in hopes of catching his eye. He was maybe sixteen or so and had the kind splendid allure that adoration bestows on people who are used to being lured into other people's beds.

When we reached the fifth floor he happened to glance at me and immediately understood the reason I was staring at him. I got out of the elevator, my heart beating wildly. There was a large red leather bench on the landing on which I sat after refusing to accompany my uncle inside the office of some insurance agent or other. I scanned the corridor for the person whom I had already decided to call my friend. It was the kind of friendship that was somewhere in between life and death; the world embodied in a blue uniform. . . . I invented a marvelous story in my head while seated on the bench. On the way here we had passed by Trinity Church, whose garden, my uncle had told me, had only been built at the end of the last century. I transformed this church into my palace and the square before it into a fortress. The towers became prisons filled with various torture chambers. In one of them the elevator operator was being whipped while spread-eagle and naked. It was up to me to save him! I leapt from the window, the elevator operator in my arms, without quite understanding what it was about my daydream that made it unlike real love stories.

The elevator went up and down often, and through the open grate, the operator caught my eye each time he passed. At last my uncle came out of the office, and once more I found myself beside my friend. On the floor below a few other people got on, which meant that I had to move over, closer to him. Our hands touched. The way down seemed to last an eternity, but we didn't move. Anyone could have seen our intertwined fingers, but we couldn't have cared less. This was an example of attitude: a sign for no one but us that still flew in the face of everyone else! The elevator was taking me to hell, my pride be damned. I got out of it with death in my soul, unable to look back. Although I never saw that boy again, the memory of him was one of my strangest feelings of love. For months afterward he was the knight in a blue uniform with shining buttons that inhabited my dreams.

Young people are addicted to meaningless gestures and hopeless desires. I can think of a million examples from my own life. At school, there was a certain way of standing up for one's rivals. I remember that I had spent hours in the library before taking the baccalaureate exam, trying to learn everything about a particular period of French history. I had even gone so far as to read the secondary sources recommended in the bibliography of the textbook that I was using to prepare. My memory wasn't letting me down, and by the day of the test I knew a lot more about the subject than I needed to. I was ready for a complete and total triumph. I made the mistake, however, of mentioning this to a classmate who, like me, was hoping to get the highest grade on the exam. I told him about everything I'd learned. On the day of the exam, I was seated next to him coincidentally. Instead of cheating off him, I read what he wrote and left those answers off my own test to help him without him knowing it. He got a higher grade than I did. I couldn't give a damn about prizes and stuff like that—not when the competition has such a handsome face!

It is doubtlessly the love of theater inherent in all young men that occasionally obliges them to take stock of themselves in the mirror by playacting a role somewhere between glory and death. Like most boys, I had pretended to be Romeo, and Hippolitus and lots of other Greek and Roman gods as a kid. Little by little I left behind these heroes to assume a starring role in a drama more obscure than theirs that had no hope of a deus ex machina to prevent an all-too-human ending. This is what getting old is all about. Some people would call this drama faith; for others, it is the meaning of a life to which they desperately cling. For me, it wasn't love, but the end of love, and when I say the end, I mean the goal of it. Nothing seemed possible for us after this; it would just be living a lie. Society made me sick with its stupid prejudices, its respectability. I resented people trying to assert the principles that they had constructed on life's emptiness.

With Pierre, I didn't cheat: I loved him so intensely and in such a new way each day that each time I saw him it was as if I stood before someone else. I spread my arms to embrace happiness, but was unable to accept it, just as my love was unable to know happiness. My weakness grew out of the romanticism in which I submerged myself. Even during the most deliriously happy moments, when embraces and sighs are accompanied by an almost physical intoxication, I still wanted to know if there was something else. I wanted to know if we could surpass our present sensual tenderness. By the time I had understood that this was useless, it was already too late. I was living in a mythic labyrinth whose exit was death. Had we been even slightly more diplomatic, we could have continued living at home. The passage of time would have brought to our relationship the kind of legitimacy that only time can lend. I, however, preferred absolutes, and so kept planning our exile.

The deck seemed stacked against us, as the ominous signs that I noticed clearly indicated. First I saw an owl flying at dawn. I had gotten up early and was looking through the window at a lone star still shining in the early morning sky. The bird was flying low, skimming the tops of the trees, above the shady area in the sunlight. All of a sudden it fell from the sky and landed on the gravel of the driveway below. Did the first rays of the sun blind it in mid-flight? Stunned, it limped toward the shade of a tree, under which it remained, immobile. The sight of this really perturbed me, so I called Pierre. He got up, and we stood together on the balcony watching this bird of prey lost in an island of night that was being devoured, little by little, by an ocean of light. The fallen bird frightened me. Pierre made light of it, but I could feel inside that I was right to fear the sudden diminishment of this nocturnal power. It was as if it represented some dark force in the brilliant sunshine of our friendship. The fall of the bird was the first ring of the ominous bell of destiny. We turned from the window, and pushed the image from our minds.

Around noontime as I was going downstairs for lunch, the memory of what I had seen that morning came flooding back. I amused myself by voluntarily exaggerating its importance. I was at the top of the stairs, which were covered by a pale green carpet. I would make my peace with fate: if some other green object appeared before me before I had completely descended the stairs, then everything would work out. Our departure, our destiny, everything would be all right. I was completely sure of winning my bet because there was green all over the house. As I went down, however, the first thing to cross my path was Pierre, who was wearing a red T-shirt. The red of love thus overwhelmed the green of hope. This is what I told myself because this is what I wanted to hear. There was, however, some other, more sinister interior voice whispering insistently in my ear. Despite my best efforts to silence it, it commandeered my lips and made me say, "Red is the color of blood, the color of blood . . ." The whole thing made me lose my appetite, although it probably looked as though I was just being difficult since I was able to push it from my mind and eat something by the time dessert was served. My cousin was flattered by my recovered appetite, which she thought was the result of her cooking. She expected compliments since she always made a point of satisfying our desires.

The rest of the afternoon passed uneventfully. We took a short walk, but went back to the house early; Pierre had some things to take care of and I wanted to take a nap so as to be in full form for that evening's festivities. At nine, I was still lying down thinking about Pierre and the time that we had spent together. The beginning of the vacation seemed to mark a new period in my life. Everything that had happened before then bore no more relevance to my current life than it would have had I believed in reincarnation. Pierre blew into the room: "You're not even dressed," he said. "Come on, get ready. At least get in the shower."

I scrubbed myself hard under the running water. Pierre was singing some song or other in the next room. I had no idea what time it was. Time didn't matter to me; in fact, I despised it. Impulsively, I refused to accord it any place in my life, perhaps in an effort to prolong the happy times in my life. I had smashed my watch on purpose, since I didn't want to have that stubbornly self-confident tick, tick, tick dictating the movements of my heart.

I looked at myself in the dresser mirror several times from different angles, and even used a hand mirror to try to see my profile, which I then carelessly put on top of the shirt that I was planning to wear. When I unthinkingly grabbed it, the mirror went flying and smashed into a million pieces on the tile. Pierre came running and asked what the hell I'd done. Although I was naked, he told me to pick it up. He found my clumsiness amusing, but I took the broken mirror as a warning. Human nature's propensity to imagine the worst made me think that our fathers were going to surprise us in some inopportune position, or that the moped was going to get a flat, or that the police were going to harass us, or something even worse. Maybe it meant that we were going to run out of money, or that someone was going to turn us in after we'd run away . . .

I got dressed. My slightly faded polo made me look really handsome. Dressed as a young Florentine, Pierre was the spitting image of Romeo. Just before leaving, I spent a few minutes putting away the books that were strewn about the room. It suddenly occurred to me to open one at random to find the answer to my questions and to calm myself down. When I came across a volume of Shakespeare, I decided that this was the book that would tell me what I needed to know. I opened it haphazardly and put my finger on the page without looking: "Ah me! how sweet is love itself possess'd, when but love's shadows are so rich in joy!"

I threw the book down. What the hell did that mean? Was Pierre but a shadow when each night I held him to my body? Stupid old actor, offering me one of his plays about love expressly for the purpose of mocking me and stopping me from being happy. To hell with Shakespeare! The dead are wrong. I will be happy, even without your promises. I don't need your Romeo in order to love my own.

I took the book next to it off the shelf. It was by Dante. Because it was 10:19, I decided to add the two numbers together and read page twenty-nine. I opened the book, and counted exactly halfway down the page:

"E caddi come corpo morto cade."

(And I fell, even as a dead body falls.)

This made no sense. The poets were crazy! How could I have been so stupid as to look for answers from them? The imaginary world that they invented had nothing in common with my seventeen-year-old heart. But I was still dying for a glimpse of the future. Where to find it? Pierre told me to hurry up. I told him that I'd meet him there, and went into my father's office.

It was weird being in there while he was away. Every time I went into this room, it felt as if I was entering the Minotaur's maze. My upbringing had been strict—when my father had bothered to notice me at all, that is. I would have liked to take some sort of revenge on him, but I didn't have the time to think of anything. I spied a Bible that was sitting on an end table, placed there more as a decoration than as an object of devotion. I grabbed it, opened it with my eyes closed, and stuck my finger on the verse that would tell my heart what it wanted to know.

    I opened my eyes and read. The prophet was also shrouded in mystery, and didn't do anything to calm my fears. I was an idiot to trust these stupid books. I just needed to catch up to Pierre, and forget my worries. Under my finger the verse that it had chosen marked the incomprehensible response of the oracle: "Behold, I have taken out of thine hand the cup of trembling." Taken literally, this might have had something to do with drinking at the surprise party. But why was "taken out of thine hand" in the past tense, since I was just going there? I left the house quickly and ran so as to catch up with Pierre underneath the trees. I followed him, momentarily furious with those above, whether poets or prophets. How dare they refuse to predict that the future would be anything but beautiful romance for a lover like me! In truth, I was already used to this sort of foreshadowing. How many times had I dreamed of the future while slumbering? I had fought all my battles with Pierre while asleep; at night we were enemies who fought each other. Every dream finished the same way. He would always open his arms to me. And then, my dreams came true . . .

    Once I had a dream in which I fell and fell for hours. I had been sleeping next to Pierre. Instead of swimming to the surface from the depths of my nightmare, I continued downward toward the foot of the bed, and then further, falling freely, endlessly. The sky through which I fell had been rent in two, as if by the sun, which had already disappeared over the horizon. All around I could see the image of myself repeated endlessly: I had brilliant wings of which any bird would have been jealous. We were a thousand archangels, all with identical faces. On the other side of the sky, fiery swords smoked and burned. Suddenly I was fighting my other selves. The clouds were covered in blood, and the sun seemed to be soaking it up like some fiery sponge. The clash of our weapons made sparks everywhere. In the middle of my battle, I realized that all of the different reflections in me were covered in shadow. The sky was splitting in two. I heard a voice identify me as a rebel, and then I began to plummet anew. I fell for what seemed like an eternity, always pursued by the accusatory voice that was at the same time inflected with sadness. It was as though it was calling me a rebel out of love . . .

The music reached our ears just as we got to the garden gate. The only access to the Decazes' garden was from the back of our own. This is because our house wasn't far from the road whereas theirs was quite isolated by a wood of beeches and high walls that came right up to the edge of my uncle's vegetable patch. Going this was way wasn't really any shorter, but we could enter unnoticed, which is exactly what we wanted to do. Our neighbors' driveway was filled with cars. Couples strolled nonchalantly among the trees, seemingly oblivious to the party that they left behind them. The moon opened its melancholy eyes and pursed its lips. We approached the house.

Michel and his sister welcomed us at the bottom of the front steps. We caused a sensation as we mounted the stairs. Pierre had donned his mask. People made way for us as we entered the room. The chandeliers had been decked with colored tapers. After our moonlit trip from the house, their light dazzled me. When I was at last able to make things out clearly, I saw that Pierre had disappeared. I was in the middle of a circle of strangers. They were drinking, playing cards, and having a good time. The mood of the small group into which chance had cast me was, however, somewhat more sinister. Elsewhere in the room people were dancing. No one had removed his mask; I was the only person without one and I felt self-conscious. So, I started to drink. Several boys stroked my cheeks, supposedly for the purpose of admiring my makeup. I told them that I was just naturally tan, and wasn't wearing any. They told me that I looked good, and I began to accumulate admirers. It's true that the warm night had made me forget my worries completely. There were punch bowls of wine punch in which pieces of fruit floated. I was still thirsty, and people kept offering to refill my cup. If I had stopped there, or rather, if I had been serving myself, nothing bad would have happened. They took turns, however, handing me specially prepared, extra-strong cocktails in order to get me drunk. They succeeded, too, since I wasn't used to drinking that much alcohol.

Even though the chandeliers filled the living room with a bright light, in the library in which I found myself, the lighting was subtler, if not downright dim. The gloom augmented the falling sensation I was experiencing. I felt as if I were sinking in quicksand despite the fact that the open window next to me gave a wide view of the garden. I went outside for some fresh air. Instead of sobering me up, the night breeze engulfed my body like a second skin and made my head turn at an alarming speed while at the same time compressing my chest with its leaden hand. I grabbed on to a small railing of forged iron at the bottom of the stairs to hold myself up. I stayed there until I got hold of myself, and then decided to go back inside. There was a piece of pointed metal that caught my pants pocket and tore my trousers. I reappeared in the library with a scandalous amount of skin showing through a gaping hole in my pants. I continued on inside the house, convinced that no one would notice if I stayed in the shadows. Michel appeared with the group of people I had left when I went outside.

"Hey! You're not dancing?" He sounded so surprised that the girls in the group suddenly took an interest in me. I told him that I didn't like to dance alone and that, anyway, I only knew the wildest kind of native dance. I said all this idly, as though I didn't care.

Several voices started demanding immediately, "We want to see. Show us what kind of wild man you are." They began chanting, "Wild man! Wild man! Wild man!" I realized that I had no choice. I told them I felt roped in, and so we went outside in front of the front steps. Of course I was already drunk, so my crazy dance made my head spin even faster. I was getting hot and decided to take off my shirt and dry my chest with it. I was going to put it back on, but someone grabbed it from my hands. I told them I'd had enough, but they demanded more, chanting and clapping, "Wild man! Wild man!" Other people were drawn by their cries. I was totally out of control, spinning wildly. I almost fell over, but a guy emerged from the crowd to catch me, which made everyone laugh. He took off his shirt as well and threw it into the crowd. Then he grabbed my wrist and started to spin us around in a circle. The guy had taken off his mask. I saw that he had a muscular neck and a sensual mouth. I dried my sweat with my forearm, feeling tired. I could tell from the way the guy dealt with me that he was maybe twenty years old. He didn't hide the fact that he was planning to have some fun with me. The trees and people around us kept spinning; a luminous rectangle of a brightly lit window that kept flashing before my eyes made me feel as though I was going to scream.

Just when I thought it was over, the guy turned toward the crowd and announced that he was going to do an Apache love dance. He pulled me against him, put a hand on the part of my skin exposed by the rip in my pants, and stroked his fingers in such a way that made his desire plain to everyone. I was dizzy and let him do what he wanted. Someone shouted, "Take off his clothes! Don't Indians always dance naked?" The guy held me between his knees and started to paw at the buttons of my pants with his free hand. I didn't react, only aware of the intoxicating effects of both the guy and the night, one of which held me brutally in his arms, while the other impregnated my limbs with a sweet suppleness. Then, in just one second, everything changed. Someone shoved someone else and punches began to fly. Pierre had thrown the dancer onto the ground. All of a sudden my head was clear. The guy got up, wanting to fight. He threw himself on Pierre. Wanting to separate them, I went to help Pierre, who pushed me out of the way.

I shouted at the guy that he was chicken, and should fight me instead. He redirected his furor from Pierre toward me, calling me a tease and a sissy. We moved deeper into the garden toward a clearing where we could really have it out. The party raged on around us. We fought bare-chested while the others, who had started to lose interest, returned to dancing or to making out under the trees, their shadows mixing with those of the leaves, which rustled in the moonlight. Soon we found ourselves alone in the moonlit clearing. Although the guy had a handsome, sensual face, I only had eyes for Pierre and refused to see his beauty. The moon was so bright that his face must have been clearly visible, but I saw him as a shadowy figure, so dark and sinister did his eyes appear to me. His shoulders practically glowed, but I saw an enemy standing before me, someone who doubtlessly was going to beat the hell out of me.

We attacked each other. He grabbed me around my waist and squeezed hard, trying to pick me up and force the air from my lungs. I grabbed his neck to strangle him. We made a strange pair, illuminated by the cold light of the moon as we were. Everyone else had abandoned us, if, in fact, they hadn't simply ceased to exist altogether. We rolled about on the ground, but neither of us could gain the upper hand. I was on top, and then he flipped me over. We took turns dominating each other, depending on who was more energetic or more devious. I didn't relax my grip around his neck until I couldn't squeeze anymore. I couldn't catch my breath. As things started to go black, I began to wonder if this was it. Maybe this guy would kill me.

Had we not been so intimately involved, I would have had his body on the spot. Only the smallest change in perspective would have transformed our battle into the duel of two lovers. At times we were immobilized, his mouth pressed against my cheek, my eyes watching his muscles start and jerk as they prepared themselves for a final victorious effort. The silent sheen in which the moon dressed our sweaty bodies transformed us into luminous statues. The only sounds to reach my ears in the midst of our silent battle was the heavy breathing of my opponent and, under that, the irregular pulse of either his blood or my own—I wasn't sure which. At last I disentangled myself from his grip. With my back on the ground, I caught his head between my thighs and crushed his neck with such force that he stopped struggling. Despite his powerful chest and muscular arms, he couldn't move an inch. All of my strength is in my thighs. He used his hands to try to pull my knees apart, but being unable to do so, collapsed onto my calves. I accepted his surrender. His head rested against my crotch, as pale as a death mask in the moonlight. I relaxed my legs and jumped up. He remained on the ground, his skin as white as the moon.

We had changed the fundamental order of things. We held hands as I helped him up. Once again we saw the branches swaying back and forth, and heard the low murmur of the wind drown out the sound of our racing pulses. He went back to the group and their fun; I returned to Pierre and Michel, who were by themselves waiting for me. Pierre grabbed me by the neck, pushed me against the trunk of a tree, and gave vent to his jealousy. His resentment pushed him to say things that he had never said before and never should have said. He told me that he wanted to kill me. With his free hand he grabbed hold of my chin so that he could hit me in the face. I was already worn out, and so did nothing to defend myself. Even though Michel stood next to us, Pierre hit me savagely. His love was so possessive that he couldn't even accept the thought that there might be someone else. In his mind, I had to be blind and deaf to everyone but him. To tell the truth, this was all right by me. It was my fault. I had provoked him. In just a few instants, Michel had already learned more about the nature of our relationship than years of friendship would have revealed to him. We left him in the garden and headed for home.

Although my face was already swollen and red, I could tell from the way that Pierre opened the barn door that he was far from finished with me. There was a long riding whip hanging on the wall. Although Pierre had never used it before except when actually riding, as soon as his eyes fell upon it, he grabbed the thing and ran it over my skin. I shivered. This caress, which I knew was but a prelude, terrified me. Pierre was amused by my fear, and without a word began to punish me for it. I didn't think he would stay brutally angry for long, and resolved myself to suffer until he was calm and in love with me again. His blows continued, however, and with such force that my courage couldn't hold up long. Soon I couldn't hold back my tears, and tried to press myself against him. He pushed me away and continued to thrash. He hit me on the shoulders, the stomach, the hands: anywhere and everywhere.

All of a sudden, however, I became as angry as he was. Was I supposed to be merely the object of his rage or of his amusement? How could he still love me and beat me like this? The night was going to teach me just how much more violent love can be than hate, and how the true color of love is blood.

I caught the crop with one hand as it flew through the air. I made Pierre drop the thing, forcing him to fall to his knees in the process. It seemed as though I had suddenly acquired all the might of Pierre's rage, and so I was easily able to drag him over to a post and tie him to it. Now it was my turn to show no pity. I would beat the anger out of his body. I forgot, however, to take my own anger into account. Little by little, as the whip kept connecting with his back or his ass, the shame that he had caused me in front of Michel transformed itself into the anger that rose inside me. I heard myself punctuating each blow with the names that his unmerited distrust had made him call me earlier: "You fucking bastard! That really hurts, doesn't it, you piece of shit!" My voice trembled; I was no longer in control of myself.

V

Slowly the sky is beginning to lighten. I have killed Pierre. Through the crack of the door, I can just make out the inky sky. The clarity with which the only star still visible shines is the advent of a beautiful day. Pierre is lying on the ground, his head leaning on his shoulder, almost as if he were asleep. He is dead and I know it. I just don't want to see the blood running down his damaged knees, or trickling from his lips to his Adam's apple. His naked body is so pale that by comparison it makes my bloodied hands seem to glow with some sinister force. I wait. I've been waiting for hours for the first light of dawn, when the birds will start to call and all of a sudden Pierre will emerge from his stillness. We're leaving today as planned, because, well, it was today that we were supposed to leave. Dead or alive, Pierre is still mine. I'll put his clothes on in just a minute.

I can't look at him, even though his eyes are shut and can no longer show my reflection. I know he wouldn't blame me because he loved me, because he still loves me. How can I be so sure? But I am sure, even if I only have his inert body to prove that everything is and will be the same as it always was. We lived at each other's side for so long with all the expected moments of silence and joy. We made it through times of sadness and frustration. Side by side we hoped and had fun.

Thus, the cruelest recollections become sweet when a time of loneliness arrives. Memory is a powerful magic that has the power to transform even the most painful moments. Nothing had changed, even though nothing was the same: this is the nature of death. Someone who is dead is just someone who is far from us; it's not time, but rather distance that stands between us.

Please, oh please, let me remember those dream hours. Remind me of when we slept in the same bed with our legs intertwined, united in each other's arms under the covers that protected us from the night's chill. I deserve to remember this moment, if it is true that I can be destroyed by a simple mistake that I will be condemned to relive eternally—at least until the supreme darkness returns my love to me! I don't want the day to come; it will always be night in this barn. Pierre loved the dark, which is why I have laid him to rest in this shadowy bed. I don't want the light to tousle his hair, to watch over him, to see how deeply he sleeps. Get out, luminous inquisitor! This body belongs to me!

I killed for the sake of love. I won't forget one moment of that night. Pierre was tied to a post; I had bound him at the wrists. He struggled to break free, but the ropes held fast. His anger diminished with the first blows, and he tried to make a joke of it. He knew I was going to stop. I deserved to get back at him, but I'd already shown him how much he'd hurt me. He was sorry. Then, when I didn't stop, he became quiet. I continued to hit him with all my strength, which was exactly the way he usually hit me. I can still hear the grunts that I made as I strained to access every last reserve of my animal savagery.

It was dark in the barn, but there was enough light for me to see that Pierre could take it. The riding crop was a long dark shaft, whose mean whistle attested to its reality. First it complained like the night wind as it fights through the trees. Then, when the doublet and tights of the costume still worn by Pierre offered his bare flesh to me, it growled with groans of love as it set itself into his swollen flesh. Pierre moaned, but didn't flinch. He was tied in such a way that he couldn't stand completely upright, nor could he kneel on the ground. The shadowy barn hid his welts from me. He laid his head on his wrists; was he crying already?

I was working so hard that my mouth was half-open. Pierre's body appeared before my eyes more clearly than had we been standing in the noonday sun. The whip had become my arm. It was an extension of my entire body, as if it were I who was wearing down this back and these thighs that were the object of my violent devotion. I was no longer a man, but rather a whip's blows with the face of a man. I would as soon have beaten myself. I was standing above Pierre, the whip pressed into my hand, trying to resist the urge to throw myself on the body. Love hid the blood that ran down Pierre's calves and into the hay. Love, that executioner who had taught me how to torture, channeled its furor from my arm into my loins, highlighting the splendor of this reclining boy who seemed to be waiting to be violated. Without putting down the whip, I approached the body. I was so thickly covered in sweat that I appeared to be made of metal. My cousin's sweat smelled of love; I didn't realize that it was actually blood with which he was covered. I bit him on the neck with my entire mouth. His smell—the smell of his underarms, his chest, and his crotch—invaded my nostrils and made me lose my head.

My hands recognized Pierre as they slowly stroked his shoulders down to his belly. When I picked him up in order to kiss him, the strong smell under his arms, a mixture of desire and fatigue, made me swoon. Pierre and I became one; it was as if I was inside him and together we were being held in the arms of love. I held my cousin's waist between my palms in order to make him stand on his own two legs. He remained slightly hunched over because of the ropes. I possessed him, alarmed to see happiness slipping from my grasp with each passing second, because I knew that I was going to make him cum, and that cuming would kill him. Pierre tried to hold back. He tensed his muscles, but once my desire had proved itself stronger than his, gave up and let a profound softness take hold of his body. I was blinded, my hands unable to feel anything. Thoughts raced through my mind with the violence of runaway horses.

I hugged his stomach from behind and unleashed an organ of brutality upon him. When I paused to rest a moment, I realized that he was crying. I understood that it was from pain, but that it was his turn to learn what it was like to be taken over by the person who loves you, although part of him still resisted this particular pleasure. He would have killed me had I untied him. A thousand times an excess of rage overtook me. A thousand times an infinite ecstasy had lifted me off the earth and robbed me of the one who brought me this painful joy. And then I withdrew so as not to give in to these murderous desires. Pierre was the only person that I had allowed to possess me, and I realized at last that it was the same for him. I murmured, "I adore you." I grabbed his sides. I wanted not just my sex, but also my entire body to own this skin, this pain, this weakness. My heart mixed my dreams with my slowly increasing pleasure. Pierre gave himself to me little by little, with a strength completely independent of all feminine sensuality. He was a man giving in to his need.

I went completely mad, and each thrust of my hips became exaggerated and incoherent. I thought I was leaving my body behind as I put the distance of stars between us, but a small moan returned me to him. I took his head and tipped it back. My half-opened mouth found his tear-stained eyes. My tongue sought out his ears and then his mouth from which his hot saliva ran into my own. I stroked his face with both hands, covering him with kisses. And then I strangled him.

The storm of pleasure struck me with its lightning. For a long time afterward—or at least, so it seemed—I felt its thunder exploding in my body. My flesh went rigid as a cadaver's as I pressed into my cousin. I heard nothing, saw nothing, felt nothing except for the night itself.

When the storm had dissipated, Pierre begged me:

"Untie me, Gerard. Untie me. I'm going to die . . ." I realized that we had made love in his blood; I untied him so fast that I lost hold of him. He slipped and fell onto his back. He couldn't hold himself up anymore, so I spread him out facedown on what remained of our clothes. The sadness that always follows orgasm made me feel as if I were a murderer. I threw myself at Pierre's feet. I raised his head, and kissed his cheeks as if he were a child.

He spoke to me at last. Each word drove itself into my heart as if it were a knife. "I'm going to die, Gerard. I still love you, which is killing me as you've killed me. . . . That was what I wanted, I guess. I can't tell you how much I still love you: I see it like a deserted island, floating in the middle of a bloody sea. For a long time I have loved you like a brother and like a lover, for such a long time that the memory . . ."

. . . And he told me everything that he held in his heart, almost as if he had been daydreaming on the banks of a river on a sunny day. He told me at random of all the things he remembered: the hours we'd spent together in school. Our evenings in Paris. The look of a tree at dawn. The presence of the other, warm like the sun.

"The sky was a deep royal blue . . ." he whispered in the barn during the final hours of the night. And so the story of two boys by the side of the river began again with the same irresolute force that stirred in those whom nothing has yet united. I learned of my love as seen through another pair of eyes. It was as ardent, as virile, and as tender as my own. His delirious ravings lasted until the first rays of the dawn. Then there was a moment of silence. Sweat streamed from his head, which I held in my hands. It was as if water was fleeing from his body. His cheeks became cool to the touch, and the grip of his fingers waned. It wasn't agony, but rather the end of agony. He had begun dying with the last lash of the whip. He spoke incoherently: "The sky was royal blue.... Last summer... last summer... and Gerard and I found ourselves alone on the road. You've got to watch out for shadows. Death carries golden apples in its hands, which it throws after us to make us run faster..." Then he seemed to come to his senses, and with great sadness said, "I'm dying, but you must keep going, keep walking in the light. I thirst for you..."

I leaned over to kiss him. His lips were so cold that they were practically unrecognizable. When my mouth left his, his head fell back into my hands as if he had fallen asleep. His heart was still. I took him in my arms, and lay on top of him. I held him tightly, but he didn't react, as if he were overcome with fatigue and didn't want to wake up. I stayed like that, spread out on his dead body, for quite some time. It was my turn to tell him about love. I told him my story in the voice of a young lover who, in order to hide his turmoil, takes advantage of the night to say what he cannot explain during the day.

I am going crazy. Hours have gone by. The sun is coming up. Daybreak has seen me lying on top of Pierre, holding him, my head on his head, my heart pressed against his. Why didn't you do anything to save him, you murderer? Love has killed love. It should be arrested and thrown into prison. I didn't want to kill anyone. Pierre should live and I should die! Ancient omens, how you tempted me! With your birds, your colors, your mirror, your books; all knew more than I did. I heard their confident answers to my questions, but I couldn't understand. Behold the trembling cup taken from my hands, and behold the love robbed from my body. It is as if the almighty is abandoning me, like a flooded river that leaves nothing but muck and destruction in its wake. How can I go on? You, omens, do you foresee another death in the near future? Dare I bet against my own fate?

A lover who has spent the night next to the one he loves can watch the day break without fear, not even realizing that it's the start of a new day. The lover whose passion is the night's prisoner waits hopelessly, unable to sleep. As soon as the horizon hints at the palest glimmer, he gets up and runs after lost time. The lover who has only memories and but a single cry to hearken death despises the night. He neither sleeps nor wakes, waiting only for the arrival of death. I am that lover. My single cry was Pierre. My body, that call.

I was breathing heavily, unable to empty my chest of the fear that was suffocating me. I had a feeling that it was useless to wait any longer. Slowly the idea of leaving began to insinuate itself into my thoughts. I knew I had to take the body with me, if I wanted him to be mine forever.... They could arrest me, kill me, whatever; nothing else mattered. I did what I had to do. It all went by so quickly that soon it was in the past. I went to the house to get some clothes. Everything was still. I chose both our clothes with care, selecting the same kind for both of us, which seemed to befit the occasion.

I took a quick shower and saw in the bathroom mirror the bruises all over my back that Pierre had inflicted with the whip. I got dressed and headed toward the barn. I had brought a wet towel with me, with which I washed my cousin's face. The blood and sweat had dried to a rusty patina on his lips, his neck, and his temples. Then, I dressed him. I had to bend his arms and lift his torso in order to get his shirt on. It kept sticking to his chest, which irritated me. For a moment, I had the crazy idea that he was still alive and was just being difficult. *He's going to wake up,* I thought, *and smile at me.* I closed my eyes and beseeched all the gods I could think of to give him back to me, sure that they would hear me. I opened them only after several moments of silence, when I was sure that nothing was going to happen.

Once I'd buttoned his shirt, I had to contend with his legs, which were even less cooperative than his arms. The hay stuck to his legs. I couldn't get the pants up over his thighs. His penis refused to go into his pants. The sun was rising quickly. I was afraid of this funereal clothing, afraid to dress a dead lover in the clothes of a live one. It seemed wrong to dress myself in the same clothes as the person I had just killed, having literally broken his heart.

Pierre looked as though he was just resting after having taken a long walk. His shoes were another trial; I simply could not get his feet in, as if they were refusing to participate in this comedy of errors. "I am dead," my cousin seemed to say. "Leave me be. I've had enough of your world. My days of walking are over. Leave me alone; I want to sleep . . ."

Eventually, everything was ready. I went to the garage and got the moped, which I barely knew how to drive. I opened the barn door only partway so that it hid what I was about to do. Next I knelt down next to Pierre, and with difficulty, took him in my arms. The dead are heavy.

I was racing against time, my memories in pieces in my head. Who was I? What was I doing? I turned over the bloody hay, picked up the pieces of our clothing, and hid them at the bottom of a garbage can. Nothing would give us away. I put a little gas into the tank of the bike, which I found in a can in the barn. Then I hoisted my cousin onto the motorbike and leaned him against my back so that he wouldn't fall off. I had to wedge him between the spare tire and the seat, and then attach him to me with my belt. He was fairly secure this way, and I'd be able to tell if he started to fall off. I don't know what providential force kept his torso upright, but it remained so, pitching slightly forward. I put some sunglasses on his eyes, so that he didn't look so strange. The speed with which I was going to drive would prevent people from noticing anything, anyway.

I didn't have any baggage, but I did have all the money that we had stolen. I was ready to go at last. The bike started easily; so easily, in fact, that it seemed to invite some future danger. I decided to go down a side alley, so as not to pass in front of the house and wake anybody. I hadn't thought about the gate to the road. Happily, someone had left it unlocked. Without getting off, I was able to push it open enough to get through. I must have looked like some kid off on a joyride. In reality, I was a murderer on the road.

I left Amboise as fast as I could, heading south. Where? I had no idea. I just had to go; where and why didn't matter. I turned on to different roads at least ten times; Pierre's body stayed where it was. I was strangely calm. The morning had brought with it the kind of restfulness that usually follows sleep. I hadn't fully realized what was happening to me.

My escape route was incredibly beautiful. Nature offered me its most gorgeous face at the exact moment when I was going to leave it. I didn't want to smell the heady odor of the wet fields, nor hear the cries in my heart: "You're in love with love. You're in love with love . . ." My love was dead; I had no choice but to kill myself. So, I admired the forests that stretched before me. The orderly trunks of the trees separated the fields of wheat like some Impressionist painting. I drove past fertile fields, whose crops undoubtedly grew tall and thick because they nourished themselves on the fruits of the dead. I passed waves of alfalfa, dotted here and there with the riotous red of poppies. Everywhere there were shining pools, valleys of flowers, capricious paths bounding over the horizon, the smell of dirt, the taste of the earth. At that moment I knew that in a few hours, I would have a mouthful of this pungent flavor.

I didn't know where I was heading, but I would keep running until death caught up with us. My blood was pounding in my heart. From one dream to another, I passed into unknown regions. The sun was high in the sky. On a village clock I noticed that it was already almost eleven. Strangely, the roads remained empty; we met no one. The world had abandoned us.

"Do you remember," I asked Pierre, "those linden trees whose branches we could touch from our window on Malherbes Boulevard? What about that engraving of the David that hung in the stairs? Do you remember, next to the bed there was a lamp that I would turn off whenever I wanted to kiss you. My books were scattered all over that room then, back when I was just dying to touch you. I'll never forget the smell of the honeysuckle, that afternoon at Coeuvres, your red sweater, or those evenings we used to spend in the garden after it had already gotten dark. Then we'd take a walk in the forest and tell each other stupid stories to make the other one laugh. What about Lycée Carnot? Or how about those long talks we'd have at night, each of us in our own bed, each of us looking through a different window and seeing different corners of the sky? Do you remember the light of July afternoons? All those noisy kids in the Monceau Park? How about the beautiful skies above the hills of Saint Cloud when the sun set? Do you remember that birthday party where, without even thinking about it, I kissed you right on the lips? What about the scariness of the Avenue de Courcelles at night, when we returned home from the movies? I was always so unhappy whenever you made plans without me. Do you remember how handsome I thought you were . . . do you remember, do you remember? And how awkward we were when we first became friends. Maybe we were already living in the suffocating atmosphere of an inescapable passion, since I was already always looking at your mouth, your neck, your strong legs. Thanks to all those imperceptibly subtle movements through which love gives itself away, like putting my hand on your arm or taking you by the shoulder, I ended up seeing your face approach my mouth, and your mouth running over my body looking for my pleasure. I had imagined my future at your side, like a straight road, without any obstacles for our affection to overcome. The blows were my gentleness. . . . You'll see, I'll pass the bac and next year, I'll learn to fly a plane. I'll take you into the clouds."

I don't know how I managed to avoid driving off the road. My instincts must have saved me at least ten times. With Pierre dead, the idea of Pierre filled in for his actual presence. I couldn't stand this for long, however, since his body weighed so heavily on me. With him gone, the power of friendship, even in death, meant that I had to die. I couldn't live in the memory of him. Everything that wasn't part of the heart now became strange to me. Life shocked me with its sweet eternal sentiments. Eternity itself is a kind of presence, I suppose. I loved Pierre, and so would never leave him. Next year it would be the earth . . . in his mouth and in my own . . .

The heat shone on the asphalt of the road. To the right the fully grown fields of grain danced a few feet above the ground. To the left, you could just see the trees beginning to turn red, as the summer slipped away, its heat and length giving way to something colder and longer.

I was lost in the middle of nowhere, a fact that I realized while contemplating the fields on either side of me. Somehow, I had wended my way into the middle of the Vienne region, by taking one small road after another, never looking at a map or paying attention to any sign. I had simply followed the horizon. Soon, it would be four o'clock. The gas can from the barn that I had used to fill the moped's tank twice already was now completely empty; I left it on the side of the road, along with the license plate that I had taken off the bike, with the crazy idea that this would mean that no one could identify us. We were surrounded by trees, which pressed right up to the sides of the road. The sun beat so strongly on the sandy shoulders that they shone like streams of stagnant water. The road alternately bent and dipped so that sometimes it looked as though I would drive directly into the immense valleys of trees spread before me.

I didn't really have any kind of plan. I'd think about it when the gas tank was empty, not before. Was this when I would meet my destiny? I ascended a hill and saw upon reaching the top of it a large stretch of road that curved slightly to the right about a mile on, and then sharply to the left shortly after that. A large tree stood at the bottom of the hill. Here was death. The road vanished behind this tree, which loomed immense and dark, its leaves veiling its face despite being illuminated in the afternoon sun. I hit the gas as I crested the hill.

Death was jealous of us. It would start by devouring our most tender parts: our loins, our lips, our eyes—everything that we'd used to love each other. By the time it reached our hearts, there would be nothing left but a cold and empty hole. Our hearts, those mute symbols of our love, would die with us.

As I raced down the road, each second bringing the end closer, I felt feverish and wanted to vomit. I sped up, lifting myself from the seat so as to round the first curve. Pierre's head moved slightly on my shoulder. A shadow crossed the road. Before me was an apple tree that stood like a black door in the middle of the road. Despite my increasing speed, I noticed as I approached it that it was covered with small golden fruit. I caught a glance of my own face in the rearview mirror, and saw that it was pale, despite my dusty, sunburned mien. I ran my hand through my hair, which was wet with sweat.

The shadow threw itself upon me, pressed me to its breast and caressed me with its tepid hands. The sound of the moped reverberated throughout the valley. I felt Pierre's lips against my neck, and looked at our faces one last time in the bike's rearview mirror. I loved him; we would live on together. My body exploded as I crashed headfirst into the shadow.

ABOUT THE AUTHOR

Eric Jourdan, born a Gemini, has Welsh, Basque, and Southern-Tyrolean ancestors. His adoptive father, Julien Green, was American. Jourdan was thrown out of at least ten high schools because of "insolence" and "indecent sexuality." At age seventeen, he wrote *Wicked Angels,* which was an adaptation of an adolescent adventure. The book was banned twice, but reprinted frequently after that. The fourteenth edition has recently come out in France. Eric Jourdan doesn't belong to anything, eschews the literary world, travels often, and writes a book now and again, when he can't help but do so. In 1984, he wrote the trilogy *Charity, Revolt,* and *Blood* at night, in only twenty-nine days. He has written more than a dozen novels, short stories, and plays in this fashion, several of which have not yet been published. Jourdan lives in Paris in the apartment in which Stendhal wrote *The Red and the Black.*

ABOUT THE TRANSLATOR

Thomas J. D. Armbrecht, PhD, is an assistant professor of French at the University of Wisconsin, Madison. Dr. Armbrecht has written about a variety of subjects in twentieth-century French literature, including articles about the intersection of literary and architectural tropes in the works of Pierre Loti. He is a screenwriter for German television and the creator of *Herz und Handschellen,* a gay-themed police series. Dr. Armbrecht's frequent travels and time spent residing abroad are often the inspiration for his writing. In 2000, he published an article about homosexuality in Turkey in The Haworth Press journal *Harrington Gay Men's Fiction Quarterly.*

Order a copy of this book with this form or online at:
http://www.haworthpress.com/store/product.asp?sku=5402

WICKED ANGELS

_____ in softbound at $12.95 (ISBN-13: 978-1-56023-548-4; ISBN-10: 1-56023-548-9)

Or order online and use special offer code HEC25 in the shopping cart.

COST OF BOOKS_____	☐ **BILL ME LATER:** (Bill-me option is good on US/Canada/Mexico orders only; not good to jobbers, wholesalers, or subscription agencies.)
POSTAGE & HANDLING_____ (US: $4.00 for first book & $1.50 for each additional book) (Outside US: $5.00 for first book & $2.00 for each additional book)	☐ Check here if billing address is different from shipping address and attach purchase order and billing address information.
	Signature_____
SUBTOTAL_____	☐ **PAYMENT ENCLOSED:** $_____
IN CANADA: ADD 7% GST_____	☐ **PLEASE CHARGE TO MY CREDIT CARD.**
STATE TAX_____ (NJ, NY, OH, MN, CA, IL, IN, PA, & SD residents, add appropriate local sales tax)	☐ Visa ☐ MasterCard ☐ AmEx ☐ Discover ☐ Diner's Club ☐ Eurocard ☐ JCB
	Account # _____
FINAL TOTAL_____ (If paying in Canadian funds, convert using the current exchange rate, UNESCO coupons welcome)	Exp. Date_____
	Signature_____

Prices in US dollars and subject to change without notice.

NAME_____
INSTITUTION_____
ADDRESS_____
CITY_____
STATE/ZIP_____
COUNTRY_____ COUNTY (NY residents only)_____
TEL_____ FAX_____
E-MAIL_____
May we use your e-mail address for confirmations and other types of information? ☐ Yes ☐ No
We appreciate receiving your e-mail address and fax number. Haworth would like to e-mail or fax special discount offers to you, as a preferred customer. **We will never share, rent, or exchange your e-mail address or fax number.** We regard such actions as an invasion of your privacy.

Order From Your Local Bookstore or Directly From
The Haworth Press, Inc.
10 Alice Street, Binghamton, New York 13904-1580 • USA
TELEPHONE: 1-800-HAWORTH (1-800-429-6784) / Outside US/Canada: (607) 722-5857
FAX: 1-800-895-0582 / Outside US/Canada: (607) 771-0012
E-mail to: orders@haworthpress.com

For orders outside US and Canada, you may wish to order through your local sales representative, distributor, or bookseller.
For information, see http://haworthpress.com/distributors

(Discounts are available for individual orders in US and Canada only, not booksellers/distributors.)
PLEASE PHOTOCOPY THIS FORM FOR YOUR PERSONAL USE.
http://www.HaworthPress.com   BOF06